DEIFICATION

BROOKLYNN DEAN

ISBN 978-0-578-84356-8

Any references to historical events, real people, or real places are used fictitiously. Names, characters places, and events are products of the author's imagination, and any resemblances to actual events or places or persons, living or dead, is entirely coincidental.
Edited by Kaitlyn Keller
Serpent Symbol design by B. Dean / Serpent Symbol image by Holly Bunn
Cover design by Steve Rice

For S, who is as perfectly brutal as he is beautiful,

and for M, who is an unending source of inspiration simply by existing.

DEIFICATION
BROOKLYNN DEAN

CHAPTER ONE
Idolatry

Handsome face, tanned skin, dark hair and eyes. The corners of his lips upturned even when he grimaced, creating the illusion that he perhaps took pleasure in even his personal pain. How ghastly and alluring equally. And how apt that reaction within her was.

This visage, so enchantingly beautiful while it performed haunting acts, was appealing in some way unexplained. Something atypical, something asexual. Something which created its own separate lens through which she might view him. A camera angle no one else could achieve.

He was the subject of dreams while being the fuel of nightmares. He was the physical incarnation of the divine, but the spiritual manifestation of everything unholy in existence. And wouldn't the devil's best disguise be one of utter beauty?

Yes, she imagined him saying softly, come with me. Follow me. And as he offered to drag her into darkness, she begged for the ecstasy of it.

The shape of his plump lips as he recited devilish incantations. The swelling of his pupils which cast his alluring eyes in darkness. It was all things pleasurable bound up in steel chains and barbed wire, held captive there by an unimaginable pain. The look he possessed, the beautiful flesh-and-blood house which contained only sin and torment; it was a dichotomy she hoped to somehow achieve, though she feared it might be something one could not attain by choice.

After all, did he choose the body to which his spirit had been attached? If he were a demon, perhaps the answer was yes, but if he were a person, then surely any choice in the matter was unlikely.

Either way, he certainly had the form anyone— human, demon, or otherwise— would desire. The flesh was such an easy target to manipulate, capture, own. She knew she'd follow him into the depths of hell itself if he so called, and she knew it had much to do with the appearance of that outer shell, that bronze skin, the shape of his hands which were not only elegant but also talented. How carefully they crafted words with pens and paper. How masterfully they carved his dark desires into flesh.

She practiced this same skill, documenting her inner-most desires which had all been fueled by him, by his face, by the lips with their pout and natural grin, by the words they formed, the manner in which they formed the words, by the voice which breathed the words into existence by means of chords and exhales.

God, she imagined the sounds of his exhales, the shape of those lips, when they breathed intensity into more intimate scenarios.

Then again, she considered, what could be more intimate than a blade thrust into willing flesh when the recipient of steel was not the performer of the violent act?

She sang his words in his rhythm as she dragged sewing needles across the flesh of her thigh, her calf, her ankle. She followed him as closely as one could in such an age as this.

His photos were in her hand, saved and stored away secretly in folders labeled "Savior" and "Destroyer". When he was violent, he saved those who might fear him, but his beauty, the ultimate tool of enticing them into deviance and destruction.

She, however, would not be swayed. Steadfast, she was resolute in her worship of him. No, it had nothing to do with desire for him, but the desire to be him. To be what he was— fearless of repercussion, giving in to every want and every need, the violence of release, the bliss of it. The amazement of what it might be like to simply be who he was, this person with a seductive tongue and handsome features who felt most alive when he brought death.

As she lay in her bed this night, his serpentine symbol in bloody rips of flesh upon her leg, she fell back into the sheets of black satin and pillows full of down.

A decision had been made. What good was passion or desire if it led only to itself? To continued inaction? To her own deviance that never saw the light of day; that had not been seen or talked about or witnessed in any way by her dark savior.

There'd be no more distant voyeurism. No glass-framed circuit boards acting as a barrier between the object of her affection and the body in which she existed.

Up close. Personal. A witness of the deviance which came so naturally to him it seemed divine. Holy. But she supposed deification was as subjective as musical taste or reading preference, or the desires hidden in the shadows of souls, performed only in the stillness of a darkened night.

Did she want to consume the gospels of the masses, the glory-to-Gods, and the so-called uplifting serenity of salvation? Of heaven? Or did she, perhaps, thrive in the violent words of horror tales and the gruesome songs of death?

A surge ripped through her spinal cord at the mere thought of it; the power. To take by the wrist a warm body, wrap her fist around it, and through a blade of silver thrust inside it her imperceptible beliefs until the physical crumbled under the force of will— well, that was enough to urge her hand into a much different action.

As she slipped her left hand down her stomach, over the elastic band round her waist, she made sure to bypass her sensual anatomy in pursuit of her thigh. His symbol still upon it in fresh, tender tears of flesh, she pressed down forcefully as she dragged her hand across the dripping wound.

Gasping inside gritted teeth, the pulling apart of sticky gashes reminded her of where she was. She withdrew her hand, lifted it to the ceiling where the smears of blood seemed as bright as candy apples against the harsh white of its paint, and she considered Halloween, then Devil's Night, then the acts her seductive savior performed for them respectively.

Her hand twitched in the thought that she might join his congregation this year, and when she imagined herself standing in the middle of a blackened road, broken streetlights flickering as they filled the air with the ominous buzzing of electric death, yielding a crowbar or some other such improvised weapon, her eyes cast in the shadow of her hood which hid her visage as well as her humanity, she let it fall back to her leg.

She sat up as she pressed her fingers into the carving, watching the way the pressure of even the smallest touch forced blood from it. Painful, pink around the frayed edges of flesh, broken open and alive.

Alive, she thought. And with her other hand, she reached for her phone. Called up her files, one of few still-working options of cellphones, and chose the album labeled "Savior." She elected the third recording from the bottom and played it.

Alluring was the voice. Calm and dulcet, nothing at all like it had been on the tape. She still had it— the tape— and it was almost time to release it from her possession. Such a pity. But at least she had the recordings that circulated in more evolved mediums; the voice recordings of his speeches, his beliefs. The prophetic, angelic, utterly divine voice as it spoke the words of truth, of fate, of demonic prophecy which gave meaning to every monstrous move she's ever made.

"Come now, children," he said, "we mustn't weep for what we lose. We must rejoice for what there is to gain, for what we become a part of."

Someone— a follower of his, but a very close one, a most-trusted one— chimed a bell. The deep, ominous tone rang out into the night air followed by the static of a gust of wind.

Torrence shook. Closed her eyes. She could feel the air if she focused enough on it; felt the vibrations of the church bell which had been corrupted.

A woman screamed on the recording. Gut wrenching, blood curdling. Fearful of death and praying for salvation, she begged him, "Please, no, please."

Again, he spoke, "Fear not." His words, exasperated and low. He'd explained this already. "All there is to lose is the body."

"Flesh," Torrence said in unison with the follower. She wished she knew his name too. She wanted to know everything.

"But what there is to gain," her savior said to the sobbing woman, who gasped in the seconds after he finished; Torrence assumed he'd grabbed her, maybe by the arm, but maybe by the chin. She imagined those hands around her own chin, digging fingernails into her flesh, bruises forming in the shapes of his fingertips. "It's eternity," he said to her, so lovingly. Torrence imagined a glistening of tears at the brim of his deeply hazel eyes. Power oozing out of him in that way. The depths of his soul, of his knowledge, escaping his lips through his words and his eyes and through his tears. "Don't you want to be eternal?" he asked, but he knew the answer even if she didn't.

"N-no," she sobbed still.

"Yes, you do," he said, and another gust wind blew static into the speaker.

"Please," she cried, but her fate had been sealed.

She represented charity. She was a virtue.

"It had been decided," he said calmly, the distance of his voice coming closer to the recorder now, indicating to Torrence that he must've stood again. "Long before you were ever born."

"What?" She gasped, confusion as clear in her shaking voice as fear, but Torrence knew what he had meant. Torrence knew how brightly this woman must've shone, and how that shining, virtuous aura must've called him to her. The woman cried, gasping, questioning him. "What does that mean?"

Abruptly sharp screams replaced her breathy voice. She wailed and moaned and begged him to stop, but the sound of a blade tearing into flesh continued on.

No sound came from the savior until the screaming stopped. Over the gurgling and weighted breath, he panted, "Greed..."

"Cures liberality," Torrence said in sync with at least three followers on the recording. She'd already cured this virtuous virus herself, but reliving his versions of these sacrifices wasn't instruction, not anymore. Now it was closeness, connection, a ritual performed by many but only functioning for two.

The sound of dead weight falling to the pavement thudded in the speakers of her phone. Again, the bell tolled.

A groan came from her left, and Torrence looked up from her own wounded flesh.

"I really hate that one," War said, rushing a towel across his dripping hair. His lips curled as if he could smell the corpse decaying the savior's feet. Torrence hadn't even heard the shower stop.

She turned the recording off. It was almost over anyway. "Which do you prefer, then?" she asked, rolling onto her stomach, discreetly wiping the blood from her hand onto the dark sheets of her bed, and looking at him playfully.

"None of them," he said, still working at his hair with the towel.

"None?"

"No."

"Come on."

"You come on, Tor," he said, stepping closer to the bed. "It's repugnant."

"It's not repugnant," she said, almost offended by such a remark.

"It is," he argued, muttering. "Crying, screaming innocents being tortured—"

"Innocents," she repeated disdainfully, brows lifting in surprise at the word-choice.

"The storyline doesn't even make sense."

"It makes complete sense, actually," she said, her tone rising, "if you listen to all of them."

"I'm not so sure hearing even more poorly-acted ravings of a crazed murderer killing people for being too kind or too chaste will make it make sense."

"Poorly acted?" She raised a brow.

"Fine, the actors are good." War shrugged a shoulder, then a chill shook down his spine. "I will never understand horror as an art-form, I suppose. So much destruction and chaos, so much pain. And I certainly don't understand why he targets the victims he targets."

"You don't?"

"Good people, Tor. No, I don't."

"And you call yourself a Catholic," she said, sitting up now, eyeing the way her black towel hung loosely on his delicate hips, just below the brand-like tattoo next to his bellybutton. Nothing else separating his body from her eyes save for the single pendant he wore. His taut frame, small waist, perfectly shaped torso, all exposed and so fragile; so easily ripped or torn, so easy to break or make bleed.

"I don't know what my religion has to do with it," he said. Tendrils of wet hair separated from themselves as they fell into his eyes. Glistening, the varying baby-blue and pale-pink tones lost in a sea of softened gold appeared to sparkle, as if he were an otherworldly being ready to re-enter the kingdom of heaven. His head lowered, and he lifted a hand to it, brushing back those crystalline locks from his vision. Droplets of water fell around him, catching the faint light of her phone screen, creating the illusion that his radiant skin was shimmering.

"Well," she said, grinning, "the focus is not your religion, it's mine."

"I wasn't aware you had a religion." He chuckled gently, eyeing her. "At least not one outside yourself."

"An anti-religion," she said, pursing her lips, considering it. "Anyway, the first recording is the message, the true path to salvation."

"Murder gets you closer to heaven?" he asked.

"Certainly not heaven," she said. "Salvation."

"This is supposed to clarify?"

"It would without your interruptions," she said. "The first recording is the message, a repeat in some ways of the very first piece of this story— the video tape." She paused, exhaling a hint of frustration. She was hesitant to call the prophecy a story, or to continue pretending that these sacrifices were works of fiction. "It serves as affirmation," she continued, hoping now to ease War into the clutches of her communion. "What was said on the tape was true, and what was recorded on it was real. The next seven are individual killings— humans as representations of concepts. Kill the representation, kill the concept. It makes sense."

"Sure," War said. "Literature is full of metaphor, but I still don't understand why the metaphors must be so violent. And why there are so many of them."

"There will be more," Torrence said. "I still have the video tape, if you're curious about it."

"I most certainly am not." He exhaled harshly, looking at Torrence, her beautiful blue eyes and her delicate features. What did she find so appealing about such darkness? Why had this been the path she'd chosen?

She could've been a consumer of Edgar Allan Poe or H.P. Lovecraft if she sought out something so morbid; but this Conrad fellow, this author of horrific production and storyline, it was something different from the general macabre. It felt dirty, gruesome in some spiritual way. It wasn't merely a tale of caution or commentary; it was brutal, and seemed only to glorify its brutality. Why was this so enticing to her, and further why were audible and visual representations of its story the preferred means of consumption?

"You might enjoy the audio more if you watched the tape."

"Nothing could make me enjoy the sounds of someone dying, even if it's fiction."

"What if it isn't fiction?"

"Then it's illegal and—"

"Illegal? War, look at the world around you. Barren and dangerous and grim. Nothing is the same as it was before the sky opened."

"I know that," War said, looking down at himself, at his flesh, at the branded circles of eyes and wings at his hip. "I know that far better than you realize," he whispered, guilt-ridden and full of turmoil for the very last place he should be in such a time as this was the bedroom of a beautiful woman. "But I'm afraid too many people hear merely a fraction of a very immense truth and run wild with it."

"A fraction of truth?"

"A piece of prophecy or—"

"The apocalypse isn't merely a piece of prophecy, and it's obviously quite real. Again, look around you."

"Torrence, I'm just... I'm worried you're taking it too seriously."

"Aw," she said, "you're worried?"

"I'm serious."

"I'm fine," she said. "I know what I'm doing. I'm trying to explain it to you but you won't listen, and quite frankly I'm not sure you'd accept it if you did take the time to understand it."

"I don't understand real death and real pain and real violence, so I don't want to hear people screaming and fake-dying, especially when there is nothing to learn from it." He shifted uncomfortably, looking at the towel and fidgeting with it. "It was bad enough when television was a thing... Witnessing the red concoctions splattering everywhere—" He shuddered. "I don't want to watch whatever tape you have that remains of the genre, and hearing it is even worse because you can't see how fake it is."

She stared at him, chin lowering. Gazing at his face, peering into the soft flesh of his high cheek bones, the sharpness of his jawline. What a divinely crafted being he was. What an utter nightmare such a dream could become if he were to join her or her savior or either of their respective followings. "What if I told you it wasn't fake?" She asked, her voice ripe with desire, words falling from them in passionate pulls of breath.

He looked up to her through his long lashes. Solemn and concerned, undeniably terrified, however briefly, that this Conrad was, in fact, the

Messiah he claimed to be, War exhaled a shaken pant of worry and tried to pass it off as a laugh. "It isn't," he said, attempting a smile. He tried to remain convicted in that.

"It is," she argued.

War peered into her eyes, scanning them for any semblance of humor, but found only severity; conviction. Regardless of how certain she was, he couldn't admit to himself that there was validity to this statement. The souls that started this would reveal themselves through art; he knew that. That wasn't conjuncture. That was absolute fact. But War wasn't certain much soul could have existed inside such cruel forms of creation. After a long moment of reminding himself of who he was, no matter how sinful that made this scenario in Torrence's room feel, he smiled. "Yeah," he said. "Okay, it's real."

What a pity, she thought, but it wasn't so troubling. She had all necessary pieces of her plot exactly where she wanted them. War was just something extra, something sweet— the deliciously devout cherry on top of a sinfully sinister just-deserts. "Fine." She sighed. "But you know what is real?" She grinned, eyes dancing along his torso, hipbones, the towel.

"What's that look about?" he asked playfully, eyes falling to his feet and scanning slowly, hesitantly his own body.

"It's unfair," she said.

"What is?" He blushed.

"That you come out in that towel. Such a tease."

His arms lowered, a playful exasperation on his lips. "You just had me. How insatiable." He chuckled, looking back down to the towel, taking it in both hands and touching around the seam of it. A simple smile, calm and serene on his face, he looked over to her through his lashes and locks of dripping hair. "Greedy."

She moved back into the bed, pulling the blanket around her feet and signaling for him to join her inside it.

Obeying, obedient, and not-at-all violent, he did as he was instructed. Lips, no longer curling in dismay and disgust, pressed against hers in a sensational blend of absinthe and caviar, decadent and illegal and sinfully sweet.

"Greed," she breathed against his lips, "cures liberality."

"Isn't this lust?" he asked between embraces.

"It's all of it," she said. "This is everything."

"This is sinful," he said lowly.

"It's also spiritual."

"More physical, arguably," he said.

"Don't be a downer." Torrence scoffed, brushing his hair from his eyes and smiling when it inevitably fell back into them. "You drive me insane."

"Non compos mentis," he tittered, letting his eyes close when her fingertips tickled the back of his neck. "I agree."

She smiled, watching him tilt his chin in response to her delicate pets. Such trust there was between them in this moment, this gentle intimacy. How opposite it was from her original intent, but how delectable in its subservience it was regardless. She considered briefly, as his eyes fluttered closed, if corrupting the holy was more thrilling than extinguishing it. Either way, here in her bed, beneath the tender instruction of Torrence's typically-violent fingertips, War laid unguarded, neck exposed, arteries vulnerable.

Torrence acknowledged that most people probably didn't consider their intimate partners in such a way, but Torrence wasn't most people. Torrence knew the Savior, her own personal deity, and before Torrence had begun working violence for him toward his ungodly goal, she'd been vicious for years and for no purpose.

But where her Savior made sense of certain urges, War made sense of others, and he taught her a patience she never knew possible; A patience that was necessary, especially to one so tempestuous and, quite literally, trigger-happy.

Here he was, after all, lying in her bed with her, exposed save for the unfurling towel around his hips, and he'd pulled back when she'd kissed him.

He let her touch him. He let his hands wander hesitantly along her frame. But what War saw as giving himself to Torrence was nothing she hadn't already taken from many others, some of whom still followed her into the darkness their deeds worked to spread.

She realized chastity was a part of War when they'd first met, though it hadn't mattered then, not to this purpose. He was selected for it, among other things, but there had been something magical about him— about his gleaming eyes and radiant, iridescent skin, that baby blue undertone in his face naturally highlighted by the purest pink any artist could conceive of. From a distance, he was the same virtuous soul both Torrence and the Savior wanted to destroy. Up-close, he was something of which Torrence could not have conceived, even in such as time as this.

Maybe, she considered as she continued her ministrations at the base of his hairline, there was nothing magical about him. Maybe, she questioned, letting her free hand roll across his shoulder and down the side of his back, War *was* magic. Maybe he'd been touched by some deity claiming to be an angel, maybe lightning struck him, and maybe he'd been a tarot-card-reader before the skies opened. Maybe not. Maybe he was a breed all of his own, something purer than people.

His lips curled upward gently, and he peeked at her with one eye before opening them both. "What?" He chortled.

"You're precious," she said, her fingertips still moving down his side, fluttering now at the top of his undone towel.

"You're cunning," he breathed, leaning into her and pausing just above her lips.

"I'm serious," she whispered, closing the small space between them.

"I'm slipping," he whined against her lips, mimicking her motions and caressing her side with his fingertips.

"Slip away," she breathed. "I'll take care of you."

He hadn't resigned to giving in, not yet, but he wasn't fighting her as actively as usual. She was gentle with him, tender even, and he believed her— for whatever reason considering their meeting, or perhaps because of it— when she said she'd keep him safe.

Lost in Torrence, in the palpable reverence which guided her body more gently against his than either of them thought she was capable, War let his body melt into the sensations. He kissed her, felt her, let her feel him and kiss him. His hand slipped across her hip and down her leg, stopping him; his eyes opening wide when he felt the crusting wound on her thigh. "Oh." He lifted his hand away, looking down toward it and realizing his state of dress. "Oh, God," he said. "I'm sorry."

"No," she exhaled exasperatedly as he moved away from her. "War—"

Lying on his side, his body against hers, his hand still hovering above her abdomen, War looked up to her apologetically. "I can't..." he said, biting his lip briefly. Looking back to her leg, he let his hand reach for her injury again. "But I can—"

"Stop," she demanded, stopping his hand with both of hers. He looked up to her, brows lifted gently, his lips parted ever so slightly. "I hate it when you do that," she said, jaw clenching.

"But it..." He glanced down at their connection, at the drying blood forming a swirling center shape, like a serpent, with points at its sides and head and curls extending from its top. "It looks painful."

"Being alive is painful," she said.

"It can also be pleasurable," he countered.

"When you start participating in that one, you can worry about the first."

"Tor, you don't understand," he said.

"We don't understand each other."

"We can try." He smiled sadly. All he'd been doing here was trying... and failing.

She considered arguing further, but the clock on the wall reminded her of the time. Nearly one a.m. and she had a very important meeting at three. Looking back to him, she smiled. Rolling onto her side, she pulled his arm around her waist. "Tomorrow," she said. "We can try tomorrow."

Though tomorrow wasn't promised to War. No time was dedicated to him, not even tonight. It couldn't be. Torrence had no control over the light of the virtues nor when that light would be revealed to her.

Sometimes it took weeks. Other times, mere hours. Tonight was an unholy communion, and soon it would be Devil's Night. She closed her eyes, considered the power swirling in her savior's veins, in her veins, in the communions shared by them through spirituality and fate and nothing more, and she prayed to her demonic orator that tomorrow would bring virtue to her too.

CHAPTER TWO
Manipulation

She waited until War fell asleep to leave. It was easier to slip away without his questions, his concerns. The constant "Where are you going? Why so late? With whom? Who is driving you? Why don't you drive?" It was too much to answer to someone who was so unwilling to believe the truth.

She looked to him as she donned her uniform. Buttoning high-waisted, pants above her bellybutton, Torrence considered the simple jeans he always wore, proof that it wasn't the clothes that made the man. Instead, with people like War, it was the essence of his spirit within the body which transformed merely by proximity to him even the most basic article of clothing into an opulent work of wearable art.

Curled into himself on his side, War truly was the living embodiment of innocence. So opposite the Savior, yet so undeniably appealing in the same awe-inspiring, passion-evoking, almost ethereal manner. Funny how she thought his hair, which had been drying now for over an hour, still glistened in the sliver of pale moonlight which shone into the room through the small break in her jet-black curtains. How strange he appeared, this entity of lightness and color, upon a California king of deeply black satin sheets and midnight blankets.

He was so delicate, not at all violent, and she wondered, in these moments of silent and still-visual consumption, if perhaps he was only so appealing because he was everything she never had been.

Innocent, faithful; he was good, and goodness was not something

Torrence was used to enjoying. After all, his original appeal had nothing to do with desire of him, but desire grew all the same.

As she stepped into her boots, she considered that attraction to War was not her fault. To be desired was to exist with someone like War, someone with his abilities.

Torrence tucked a cheetah-printed shirt into the leggings just above her bellybutton, running her fingers over the silky material and acknowledging the difference of sensation when the tips of her fingers touched the vinyl of her pants. The difference, she imagined, was the same as War and any regular person— any pre-opened-sky person.

The silky shirt, the regular, the old; the time before, when people were just people and there was only man and there was no god. The vinyl, the material of the times now— easily cleaned and waterproof— was the present and the future, the signs of changing times and opening skies; the time of tangible lightning and visible spirits.

She'd never asked War how he'd gained his abilities. Some people were caressed by the silvery lightning of the heavens, the lightning that accompanied falling angels, or so the stories went. Some stories claimed abilities were given to those humans who witnessed the fall of an angel, some said the angel touched a human and passed their powers to them. Other people were supposedly hit by flaming bolts of violet. Some with abilities claimed they had always had a special sight or some ethereal attachment others scoffed at, and the opening skies intensified them.

Torrence didn't want to know how War attained his gift. She didn't want to know if he'd been struck by lightning; didn't want to imagine the pain it must've put him through. She knew the angel stories were bullshit— no one had ever seen an angel in the ten months since the skies opened, and prior to that the only evidence found of biblical creatures was demonic.

War always countered that proof of demons was proof of angels, for demons were simply mutant angels who had rebelled against God, but Torrence didn't believe in God the way sweet, innocent, raised-Catholic War believed in God.

To Torrence, God was simply an idea— a thought or a sensation. God was the reminder of supposed-morality, that voice in one's mind that paused the hand of a would-be thief before its fingers could lock around an item and push it into a coat pocket. God was synthetic.

Nothing more than a personification of guilt and regret. Jiminy Cricket the Creator of the Universe, and Torrence was not going to worship an insect nor an idea.

Instead was the appeal of the adversary, of a being so sure of himself that he'd rebel against the creator of the universe; this appealed very much to Torrence.

She never liked the term "rebellious" even when they'd attached it to her in school, but the act of challenging the status quo, well, that had always been intriguing. She didn't like the things other people liked. Her fantasies always played out differently from the usual, or so she deduced. Every time someone called her deviant or tried to diagnose and drug her, she found her desires all the more appealing.

Now with the skies opening, now with the Savior so accessible, Torrence found meaning. Purpose. She realized now that her band of brothers, that every sick and depraved thought formed inside her mind then turned into action by her hands was all in wait of him, and his disgusting, divine will.

She heard the car outside. Looked to War. Wondered if she ever really wanted more from him than his virginity and chuckled at the varying ways in which she'd wanted it. Taking it seemed fun, but then, keeping it intact and using it had been appealing too. Those damn eyes. That damn face. She almost bent down and kissed his forehead, but she worried the wholesome act might twist her stomach to the point of sickness and the clock wouldn't wait for that. Timing wasn't everything when it came to ritual, but its precision was necessary. The pocket watch she held in her hand, its gold chain wrapped around her wrist like a dangling watch, reminded her of that, and so, without goodbye or goodnight kiss, she left.

She got into the car, a 1965 Chevy. Jet black. Blaring engine. Stolen by Torrence long before the skies opened and gifted to Jocelyn just before they did. Whether that timing seemed divine or demonic, Torrence didn't care. She had been planning, and each chess piece moved when and where she ordered, even those who weren't aware that they were playing a game.

"Where to, Boss?" Jocelyn grinned.

Torrence leaned forward and stuck her phone to the grip in the old car's outdated air-vent. On the screen was a photo of an old, bent map, and a path was highlighted in faint pink marker.

Her eyebrow raised and her blue eyes met the hazel tones of Jocelyn's eyes, in-and-out of glistening under the flickering street light. "If you get me there in thirteen minutes, it gives us ten to ourselves. Maybe that's enough time for a deal."

"Yes, ma'am," Jocelyn said, eyeing the the tight clothing wrapped around Torrence's frame, scanning her legs for any lumps or hidden treasures tucked inside. "I can do it in twelve."

And she did exactly that. "Eleven minutes and— Oh, there it goes." Torrence grinned at the changing minute-hand on her watch as Jocelyn pulled into the driveway of a large, isolated home. "Twelve minutes exactly."

"That should be plenty of time," Jocelyn said.

"I'd say so," Torrence agreed, removed a baggy and rolling papers from her right boot.

Torrence never partook, but she had no problem buying, rolling, and lighting up for Jocelyn. Everyone had their price; that something they'd trade anything for. Jocelyn's just happened to be drugs. Weed, cocaine, alcohol— it didn't matter so long as she didn't have to be sober with herself. And once Jocelyn dropped Torrence off with her band of merry men, Torrence didn't give a shit what happened to her behind the wheel of that car.

"Here you go," Torrence said, handing the joint to Jocelyn. She tucked the baggy back into her boot, rummaged around inside it for a second or two, then she removed a smaller one. "Since you haven't been late all month," Torrence said.

"Whoa, really?" Jocelyn smiled, tucking a fallen curl behind her ear. Torrence tossed the baggy over to her. When she caught it, she took care not to crush the two ecstasy tablets inside it. "Thanks, Tor," she gasped. "I've been dying since last month."

Drugs were harder to come by now that the sky opened. Blame it on angels walking the earth and healing the afflicted. Blame it on demons rising up from active volcanoes, killing the dealers, and snorting the shit themselves. No one knew why. For as lawless as the land had become, it was also less populated by people,and infiltrated more and more with each rip of the skies by entities which had only existed by legion in holy texts, and on Earth in minuscule numbers.

It was the end of days. Why or how didn't matter as much as survival, at least not to most people. And those left on Earth with substantial-enough bank accounts went on as normal, just added some bars to their grand windows and extra locks on their panic room doors.

"I'll give you a couple more if you help me out," Torrence practically purred. She grinned over to Jocelyn, her lips smiling gently. Kind. Loving. The best friend Jocelyn never had.

"Whatcha need?"

"When you leave here," she said, reaching into her boot and removing a piece of paper. Another map. The path highlighted this time in blue. "Go here." Torrence was careful to keep the contents of this left boot, containing multiple drugs and a switchblade, secured.

"And?"

"No one will be there. Just fuck it up."

"But I don't—"

"No one will be there," Torrence repeated, her tone sharp and impatient. She wouldn't send a druggie to do a murder's work, and she wouldn't send a murder to War's apartment anyway. Not again. And not when he was home.

"Right," Jocelyn said.

"For that you'll have to complete the task before you get your payment."

Torrence watched the windows of the mansion. Waited to see shadows passing through them. Watched the lights come on all at once before the house was consumed in darkness.

Certainly these crimes weren't easily committed here in the end of days. The activities of petty criminals were halted by the extra protection adopted by the wealthy, but Torrence, well, she'd been at this since she was seventeen, and that was many, many years before the skies opened.

Nothing stopped her, and nothing stopped her band of brothers— the handsome, vile creatures who were more monster than human, but not in any otherworldly way. Their monstrosities developed in childhood, in youthful teenage rebellion, in the suffering inflicted upon them; monstrosity of the spirit, and in Torrence, they'd found a leader.

"Do you like violence for the sake of it?" she'd asked Jason some nine years ago, approaching him in an alleyway where he stood above a concussed man. "Or is there something you seek in doing bad?"

"I like taking what I want," Jason said, turning to her, glaring.

"And what you wanted was this wallet?" she asked, lifting the brown leather billfold before her.

"How'd you—?" Jason tapped his back pocket. "You think you can steal from me?"

"You stole from him." Torrence grinned down to the man, still dreamy-eyed and gazing at nothing. "This was what you wanted, huh?"

"No," Jason said, cracking his neck. "I wanted a piece of his hot little wifey, but the dumb bitch took off. Now here you are all alone," he said, stepping against her. "Looking pretty hot yourself."

"Well, if you want some of me, big boy, all you have to do is ask," she chuckled. "But where's the fun in that?"

His brow raised. "I can see it being pretty fun," he growled. His voice husky and needing.

"I find it much more interesting when your partner is unwilling."

"Oh, you do?" He stepped closer still and this time she stepped back.

"I do," she continued, left foot following the right as she backed away. "All of that screaming, the kicking and flailing, the 'please, stop, no's."

"Uh-huh." He grinned, still slowly moving nearer.

"Uh-huh." She nodded. "Makes you feel powerful, doesn't it? Like you can do anything you want to anyone you want, and it doesn't matter what they say."

"Yeah," he agreed now, his hand falling down to the front of his jeans when Torrence backed herself against a black SUV. "I like taking what I want."

"You like having power," she said, reaching out to him, taking the front of his t-shirt in her hand and pulling him into her. "I can see to it that you have that power."

"Give it to me then," he said, leaning into her.

"Ah, ah, ah." She recoiled, lifting her finger between them. "Power isn't given."

"Taken," he said, understanding.

"You want me to show you how to take it?"

"Hell yeah."

"Right inside," Torrence said, slipping away from him. "Go on," she encouraged, "open the door."

He eyed the back door of the SUV carefully. Tempting. "What are you playing at, woman?" He glared at her.

"No games," she said. "I've been watching you. You come to this bar every night, and every night you hit on anything with a pulse. When she accepts, you bring her out here and throw her against the bricks. You choke her. Pull her hair. I see it in your eyes."

"It?"

"Rage," she said. "You want to hurt them as badly as you want to fuck them. You hate them when they comply. You want them to fight it. That's why you're always more excited when they shoot you down. That's why you go for the ones who show up with their boyfriends. You want to make someone do what you want them to do, and you want to make someone bleed. You want to make them hurt."

"Man." He scoffed a laugh. "You can't be watching people have sex out here."

"It's not always sex," she said. "You like it when it isn't. That's why I chose you tonight. That's why you're my first pick."

"Pick for what?"

"For this," she said, opening the door to the SUV. Inside laid a woman, blonde curling locks cascading around her sleeping face. Her body taut and fit and wrapped in a miniskirt. A white crop top stretched tightly across her braless breasts. Nipples hard and visible through the thin material.

"Want to talk about unwilling?" Torrence crossed her arms, leaning against the side of the SUV and looking inside. "She's out. I OD-ed her myself." Torrence looked up to Jason, a brow lifting over her devious eye. "She'll never even know."

"Now," Jason said wearily, "when you said OD-ed…"

"Just gave her a little more than she can handle. Get closer," she coaxed, "you'll feel her breathing."

Jason lifted a leg into the SUV, ready to accept the present offered, then he paused. Looking back to Torrence, he asked, "And what exactly do you want in return for this?"

"Just your loyalty," Torrence said, moving against him. She let her hand run across his muscular shoulder, down his back.

"Loyalty?" he asked, groaning when her fingers slipped inside the rim of his jeans.

"Loyalty," she said. Moving her hand away from Jason's sensitive hip bone, Torrence reached to the unconscious body in her backseat. She pushed the small skirt upward, revealing the woman's bare body. No underwear. Stripe of blonde hair. "Funny how the body reacts on instinct, isn't it?" A brow arched as she peered into Jason's eyes, her fingertips stroking gently the woman's delicate center. "She's all ready for you. Take her. Take her and devote yourself to me, and I can promise an endless supply of power."

A smirk spread across Jason's plump lips. "Power, huh?"

"Power," she said, "over anyone and everyone we decide. Follow me," she cooed, massaging his shoulder as she urged him toward the body. "Let me lead you."

He snickered, opening his belt and unzipping his pants. "Happily," he said, climbing onto the woman. "I'll follow you into hell itself."

"And so you shall," Torrence said, closing the door of the SUV and leaning against it. "So you shall."

Here, in the car, Jocelyn next to her, Torrence looked away from her brothers in the windows. Remembering that night with Jason, trying to assign a number to the countless nights she spent with him after, Torrence realized she never properly thanked Jocelyn for all she did.

Sure, she gave her pills and let her smoke. Torrence, with her seedy connections, habitual activities, and lack of compunction, provided many things to this particular pet that no one else could— at least not for so little in return.

Other deviants, other people like Torrence, they often required more than getaway cars and busting up empty apartments. The other asks, well, Jocelyn had no recollection of them, and if she couldn't remember them, Torrence figured they couldn't really hurt her.

So what if she used Jason's past with bullies against him? So what if she fed the flames of his un-admitted but entirely low self worth? This wasn't the time for therapists and healing. This was the time to take advantage of weaknesses, and use those weak-minded persons to her advantage.

She'd done it for years. Not only with Jason but with Michael, too, and Wesley and Freddy.

Michael had been easier for Michael had been younger. Torrence was twenty-six when she met him. He was a mere seventeen. Technically the age of consent in his state, and while the concept of consent never bothered Torrence, the consideration of him as a child had.

Still, he'd been in a bar, so her original assumption was that he was young enough, yes, to entice and control, but still very much legal.

She watched him for a long time. Watched him as he watched a lovely slender man flutter away from the bar and to the jukebox.

Torrence sat down across from him, entirely uninvited, but Michael said nothing. His head was tucked into his lifted shoulders, and his eyes were hesitant to move when he looked up to her.

"Whatcha drinking, love?" She grinned.

"Water," he muttered.

"Want something stronger? I'm buying."

"Can't," he said.

"Can't?"

He exhaled. Leaned back in his chair. His right hand scrubbed up and down his left. "I'm not old enough."

"What do you have— a year or two?"

A nervous smile. "Four."

Her brows raised. "Four? You're seventeen?"

He nodded.

"So what are you doing here? Why aren't you at a party or a football game or something?"

"I don't really... It's not very cool to go to those things alone."

"It's cool to come to a bar alone?"

"You're... alone," he said lowly.

"Yes, but I'm working."

Michael turned to look at the bar. His brows furrowed. Looking back to her, he asked, "You work here?"

"Nope," she said. "So why are you here?"

"Most people, even when they come to a bar alone, they don't... Leave alone." He winced. Rubbing a hand across his eye then glancing back to the man at the jukebox.

Torrence leaned back for a moment of silent contemplation. She looked over at the jukebox too, the slender man still standing against it but now with some company.

The silence between them was heavy, hanging in the air like a thick barrier separating them. Michael was more concerned that she might bully him for his obvious interest than he was about her kicking him out of the bar or turning him in for being underage.

"What's your name?" she said softly, still looking at the jukebox.

"Michael."

"When do you turn eighteen, Michael?"

"Next month." He glanced up to her, watching her, waiting, though he wasn't sure for what.

Her eyes narrowed, lips curled together. Very young he was, but very submissive. Very trainable. But very young. Too young in most ways.

She nodded. Saying nothing, Torrence rose from the table and walked away.

Michael didn't look up to her, but he heard the heels of her boots clacking against the cement floor; the sound fading as she moved further away from him.

He didn't watch her walk to the bar. He didn't see her order a drink— the same one the slender man had— and he didn't see her slip something inside it.

He didn't see the way she made friends so easily with the man. He didn't watch the man drink from the glass she'd given him.

Michael with his head always lowered, with his eyes always on his feet, saw nothing. But Torrence, she saw everything. She saw things imperceptible to most, things like the sorrow in his eyes and the pain in his lips and the story of where these emotions might have come from. If she couldn't see them clearly, she could certainly piece them together with educated conjectures. Without doubt, she saw where Michael had been looking this night, and, most importantly, she saw the reason why.

This slender guy, her newly acquired buddy, he'd seen Michael and he'd noticed the way Michael looked at him.

Torrence heard him ask Michael if they knew each other, and she heard Michael confirm that he used to be friends with the man's younger brother.

Torrence heard the words the slender man threw at Michael, heard him say that, oh, yes, that's why his brother stopped hanging around with him, and, wait a minute, wasn't Michael the one that they tied to the goalpost at Homecoming two years ago? Yeah, that was hilarious. They ripped his pants down and duct taped dildos to his ass.

Torrence hadn't liked the slender man from the time she entered this bar— call it intuition; looking back on things now, call it that same clairvoyance fallen angels intensified here in the end of times— but that exchange certainly had confirmed his disgusting soul.

She was appreciative for him though because he'd spotlighted her next target. Her gentle Michael. She knew gaining his loyalty would come in one of two ways, and she knew this piece-of-shit was the key to either. To both.

"Michael," Torrence said, causing the young man to flinch in surprise.

When he looked up to her, her arm was interlocked with the man's arm. He swayed a bit, groaned and lifted his hand to his forehead. "This is my new friend, Blake."

Michael shifted in his seat, trying to muster the strength it might take to smile. He accomplished the task, but he couldn't look up long enough to truly see the man so closely.

"I know..." Michael said, still squirming.

"Blake tells me you used to have a bit of a crush on him back in the day," Torrence said.

"He... said that?"

"Maybe I deduced." She shrugged a shoulder. "He's just not feeling well right now, and I think it's best to get him home."

"Yeah," Blake groaned. "Need to go home."

"Probably better if you come along. It might make him feel safer to have someone he knows accompanying him. Me, I'm a stranger in a bar. God knows what I might be capable of."

"Oh..." Michael stammered, but he stood. "Yeah... Okay..."

"Let's head out the back," Torrence suggested. "My car's in the lot next door."

"Okay," Michael simply said. "I should tell you though," he added as they exited the bar, "we're not the best of friends or anything."

"I know," Torrence said. "My car's that black one over there. Let's get him loaded up."

Torrence, still observing, watched the way Michael's eyes gleamed hatred as he helped the almost-unconscious man into the back of her

SUV. Perhaps there had been a time when taking Blake, as Jason had taken Jocelyn, would've been the key to Michael's loyalty. Not this night. Torrence saw Michael's lips curling. His jaw clenched. She imagined every ounce of pent-up rage might fill his fist if he were given permission to strike Blake... And she was right.

She drove them some twenty minutes out of town, and luckily Michael's shyness prevented him from questioning their destination.

"No one comes out here," she told Michael when they reached it. "This field is part of a big farmland, and they only use it every other year. A bit of fertilizer might help the crops next year anyway."

"I knew you weren't taking him home," Michael said.

"Then why didn't you stop me?"

Michael shrugged.

"You're not that shy, are you? That weak?"

"Weak?"

"You'd let a stranger drug your friend and drag him into God-knows-where? You're that weak?"

"I'm not..."

"You're not weak, Michael. I know that," she urged. "You wanted to see where I was going because you wanted to see what I would do."

"No, I—"

"Yes, you did. But it's okay. It's all right. I'm not going to do anything to him."

Michael looked at Blake on the ground. The man seemed very taken with the soil. His fingers played with it, pressed into it. He chuckled lazily. "Then why is he here?"

"Because you're going to do it," she said, pulling a knife from her boot.

"Oh, whoa... I'm not—"

"I won't tell anyone," she said. "That's why we're out here. No one will ever know. Just you and me, and this asshole."

"But I can't."

"Why? Why can't you? For the same reason he couldn't call you that horrific slur he used multiple times? For the same reason he couldn't beat the shit out of you? For the same reason he couldn't humiliate you? Tie you up and shame you? Oh, I'm sorry. He did those things. He never once felt like he couldn't."

24

Michael's lips shook, his fists wrenching. He looked down at Blake and saw him standing on that field, not lying in this one, and he saw him laughing and taunting him while he filmed his friends assaulting Michael's naked body.

"And all because you complimented him. All because you thought he was handsome." Torrence tsked as she looked down to Blake. "Maybe," she said, releasing the blade by pressing a switch. The sound cut through the stillness of the night air, causing Michael to jump. He looked in her direction. Eyed the weapon. "Maybe he shouldn't have been blessed with such a handsome face," she said, looking over to him. "Not if he doesn't appreciate it. Not if he can't appreciate someone who appreciates him."

Torrence leaned down over Blake, petting his cheek, and then she sank her blade into it.

He cried out, but the drugs were gripping him, and his body lagged.

Torrence laughed. "There we go," she said. "Better suited." She stood and looked over to Michael. "What do you think?" Her brow raised and she offered him the knife.

Michael looked down to Blake, saw the ability to enact every revenge fantasy he'd ever had— not just involving this man, but every man who'd participated in his humiliation, every man who shoved him into walls in the hallway, every man who stole his clothing from the locker room when he was in the shower after gym.

"I think he needs more work," Michael said.

"Then work away."

A shaking hand took the knife from her open palm. Michael was slow to start, but eventually, after the initial cut, he learned to let go.

Trembling hands grew precise. Tiny slices became enormous gashes. And as Michael stabbed and carved, Torrence filmed. She kicked the man.

Bending down, joining Michael where he knelt over the bludgeoned man, Torrence filmed herself unbuttoning and unzipping Blake's pants. She tugged at them, pulling them down.

"Flip him over," she said.

"What?" Michael asked, blood splattered on his face.

"Don't get all moral on me now," she said as she stood, the light of the phone still illuminating the men she recorded. "He filmed your ass. We film his." She inhaled deeply. "You still think he's hot? Wanna fuck him? Or do you wanna make that shit hurt the way he made you hurt?"

Michael looked down, tears forming in his angry eyes. "I want him to hurt."

"Then use the blade," Torrence said.

And Michael complied.

"I'm running out of time." Torrence said quickly, tucking her pills back into her boot, securing them with her tight pants. She stared at the house. She saw Micheal's now-matured form smash open one of the windows. She saw Jason hurling jewelry and coin through its bars.

Looking down to the clock, Torrence grinned.

In the calmness of the night, it was menacing, the pocket watch she held in her hand. Each tick, tick, tick of the second hand became each tick… tick… tick… of the minute hand.

Seven of them.

That's what she gave her band of brothers. Seven minutes.

If God could create a world in seven days, surely they could've destroy someone's life in seven minutes.

Tick, tick, tick.

She exited the car and approached the home.

Six minutes left, and she could hear smashing glass crumble onto marble floors.

Five minutes and the nighttime silence was broken by silverware crashing against mirrors.

Four minutes, and she turned her body to the door, whimsically kicking up her leg to take the first step toward it.

Three minutes and there was crying.

Two minutes and someone yelled.

One minute and loud pop silenced all.

And Torrence entered.

Surely, she figured, that her band of brothers heard the sound of her boots clicking against the ornate stairs. Surely they've used the one gun shared between the band to scare her victims quiet. She imagined they, her victims, were holding onto one another, cowering on the floor against the back wall.

That was where she instructed her brothers to herd them, and her brothers obeyed instructions well.

She imagined it was Wesley holding the gun in his left hand. She imagined him standing off to the same side, staring at the cowering couple.

Across from him on the right was surely Jason. Jason, who carried rusted chains and preferred the way their blunt iron rings busted open flesh rather than sliced it.

Far more brutal. Much more release.

Behind Jason was Michael, Michael always brandishing the blade he'd felt so comforted by since that first night with Torrence. Across from Michael, behind Wesley, was Freddy, Freddy who enjoyed choosing an item from each victim's home and using it against them. And the brothers lined up like this to watch her victims, to keep them on their mark.

Staring at them, threatening them with the mere presence of a gun, of chains, of switchblades, and pipes, her brothers made every cliche people have ever rolled their eyes about in cheap horror films their worst nightmare.

That was the funny thing about fiction— Everything was overused and overdone and desensitizes the reader or watcher to its violence until they're face to face with it.

Love didn't feel as good in fiction, and horror stories weren't as frightening as what real life could do.

As she ascended the marble staircase— now inside the home, now making her way toward her brothers, toward her victims— Torrence knocked her knuckles against the wall with each passing second.

Tick, tick, tick.

Knock, knock, knock.

"Ready or not," she said, removing her own blade from her boot.

"Here she comes," Wesley said slowly, and Torrence paused to picture the horrific beauty of his handsome features when his chin lowered and he smirked beneath the glassy surface of caramel-dipped eyes.

"Well, hello there, folks," Torrence said, walking over to a candy dish on the end table. "Lovely home you've got here, isn't it boys?"

The band all agreed.

Torrence removed a lollipop from the dish, unwrapped it, brought it to her lips. "Oh," she said, tossing the wrapper to the hardwood floor.

"Sour apple." She looked to Wesley, who had a menacing smirk on his luscious lips, and she lifted the bowl in his direction. "Want one, brother?"

"No, thank you, Boss." He grinned.

"Okay," she said with pep, smiling at the couple, then turning and hurling the dish against a large, gold-framed painting. It shattered, and the man flinched. "Wow," she said. "So very protective."

Wesley sneered, stepping closer. The man quaked against his wife, and she covered her mouth.

"Oh?" Torrence said, going to them. "Oh?" She bent at her knees now. "Was there something you wanted to say, Mrs.?"

She shook her head because, of course not, no, there wasn't. Torrence hated the fact that most people in the face of danger, in the dangerous face of Torrence herself, never said anything. Why didn't anyone fight? Where was the instinct? Why did it always sway to their flight responses?

"Why is your husband so flighty, Mrs.?" Torrence asked, placing her elbow on her bent knee and her chin in her palm. "It's very unbecoming of a man."

Wesley chuckled again. The others purred like kittens, sickening snarls and laughs slipping by their jagged teeth.

"What's there to be frightened of, Mr.? Not little ol' me, surely."

She looked up to Michael and sucked on the candy. He shook his head no, his eyes almost offended that she had to ask such a question, and she didn't have to. She knew the answer, but cat-like predators always enjoyed playing with their food.

She looked back to the man on the floor. "Lucky for you," she said, taking the sticky lollipop from her jaw and cracking it down on his head, twisting it and tangling his locks into it. "Michael doesn't like blonds."

Her eyes moved over to the woman. "Now, you, Mrs., oh…" She shook her head and lowered her eyes. "You see," she said in a calming voice, low and solemn, as she reached toward her. The woman recoiled, prompting a grin from Torrence because the fear displayed by prey excited her. Even the smell of their sweat was alluring when it stunk of fear.

She reached again, this time tougher and more quickly, and grabbing the woman's hair, Torrence yanked it.

Wails came from the woman, and the man cowered further, so Torrence kicked him. Too feeble and afraid to even moan, the man only bit his lip. He squeezed shut his eyes, his shaking hands moving toward the pain but only briefly. Too fearful to move his arms away from his body. What fun, Torrence thought.

She turned her attention back to the woman. "See," she said, twisting the woman's locks around her fingers, "Jason really enjoys brunettes."

She shook her head no, and Torrence smiled. Chortling, she sneered through gritted teeth, "Cute."

The woman gasped, shaking her head, pleading silently, but Torrence yanked at her hair, then nodded to her brothers.

In a rush of action, Jason and Michael grabbed at her while Wesley reminded her husband, whose eyes had widened in the violence gripping at his wife, that there was a gun aimed on him— typically a necessary reminder in moments like these, but this man, he didn't even reach a hand out to his wife.

It confused Torrence, this paralysis in the face of danger, but she supposed his instinct to protect his own life outweighed any instinct to protect his wife's.

She looked up to Wesley briefly, the stern expression on his face, the intensity with which he followed her. She didn't have to think of it— she knew— that his instincts would have always placed her safety before his own, and she wondered briefly why all people in love didn't respond to danger and their partners in such a way.

She wondered about the savior, and whether or not he found his purpose too important to risk. She considered War and his compassion. How opposite they might have been in the face of fear. How emotion-driven War might be, where Conrad would only be logic.

She looked back to the man who was shaking still, his eyes flickering up, watching his wife kick and squirm while the two men dragged her to the couch on the opposite side of the room.

Torrence's brows lifted briefly when she finally saw his eyes, and she looked over her shoulder. Jason lifted his knife to his grinning face. The woman screamed, "Please don't! Don't kill me! Please!"

"Please," the man finally whispered.

Torrence's brows raised, she smiled gently as she turned her head back to him. "Please?"

"Don't— Don't let them kill her. Please," he said.

"Oh, don't worry, Mr.," she cooed, lifting her hand and petting his cheek. "She's not the virtue we came for."

"V-virtue?"

"We've been watching you, Mr.," she said, "Watching you at work, watching you provide food for the homeless, watching you at the park, watching the way you spread seeds for the birds and help children when their kites get tangled in the trees."

His chest rose and fell heavily beneath his sweating face.

"So kind," Torrence said, lifting her hand and opening her palm. "Such kindness," she said, and Wesley placed the gun in her hand.

"Wh-what?" He shook out, whispering; his eyes darting up to the gun, then to Wesley's stoic face, then back to Torrence.

"Kindness, Mr.," Torrence said, removing her stroking fingers from his left temple, and bringing the gun to his right one. "Kindness cures envy," she said, the clicking of the safety release adorning her melodic voice, blending with the grunts of Jason, with the screams of the man's wife, with Michael's sickening cackle; an orchestra of violence, pain, and brutality surrounding them, surging through the room in moans of pleasure and cries of agony. "And we cant have that," Torrence said, pulling the trigger and painting the walls with the man's earthly form.

Torrence stared at him for a long moment, never moving. She lifted the gun and Wesley took it from her hand.

"Tor," he said.

"Yes, precious one?"

"The vial."

"Right," she said, removing a small glass bottle from her left boot. Raising it to the window, letting the moonlight shine into it, she closed her eyes.

The engraving cast a shadow on her forehead, the symbol of a serpent on same almost-coiled form as the one carved into her leg, with its seven points and large horns. "Envy," Torrence said, the sounds of screams growing softer, fading into resignation, tiring the body expelling them. "Envy cures kindness," she whispered. "Envy cures kindness. Envy cures kindness. Envy cures kindness."

As she continued her litany, the blackness of Torrence's lids shifted, crackling static of growing light altering the darkness of her closed eyes. Flash of lightning. Flesh illuminated, Torrence saw burnt oranges then deep pinks. Thunder cracked. Finally a fiery red painted the backdrop of her closed eyes, and behind her the exhausted woman's body, newly invigorated by terror, released a guttural scream.

As a bolt of lightning filled the room with violet brightness, Torrence opened her eyes. The iris of each, gone. Only white remained, white which streaked red with expanding vessels each time lightning ripped through the sky.

"Oh, God!" The woman cried.

"Yeah, there you go." Jason chuckled, still working toward his release. "Oh, God. Oh, God." He looked over his shoulder, watching Torrence, adjusting his tempo to time his climax just right.

"With this offering of virtuous blood," Torrence said, her eyes still pulsing red in time with the storm, "I invoke the violet."

As she breathed the final word, a fiery lightning blast tore across the sky. A clap of thunder shook the house, and inside its vibration, time slowed.

"Yes," she hissed, the word moving through the air in normal-time as everyone else around her moved in slow motion. She leaned forward with the vial, placing it just beneath the man's wound, and caught droplets of his spilling blood in mid-air. Catching them felt quite like a game. Move the vial from blood-drop to blood-drop, don't let any touch the ground.

"Fuck... yeah..." Jason's moan labored through the staticing air. "Oh... God... yeah..."

Loitering screams tore through the walls as much as they caressed them, sounding both near and far in the slowed time of the vibration.

Torrence's lips parted, her teeth exposed as she released her tongue from behind them. Moving against the corpse, his brains and blood slipping lazily from his body in the warp the house was trapped inside, Torrence pulled open his shirt, stabbed her knife into his chest and ripped the flesh there open.

She ran her tongue along the length of it, lapping at the dead flesh to get as much of his blood into her mouth as possible.

She stood then, still the only being able to move in the appropriate manner, placing the vial back into her boot. She turned to Wesley, whose eyes were closed— trapped for a moment inside the millisecond of a blink— and placed her hand at his cheek, caressing him gently.

By the time his eyes opened, they were staring directly into the all-whites of Torrence's eyes, and in his slowed vision, he perceived the blood dripping from her closed lips.

He started to part his own lips, but knew he would not have the time to complete the action here inside the warp, signaling instead by widening his eyes that he was ready for her.

She grinned, moving against him, pushing her lips into his and separating them in the force of her regularly-sped motions. The gentle vibration in his throat moved against her before any audible bit of his moan was heard, and instead of closing his eyes and reaching for her in this moment of intimacy, he let his finger find the trigger of the gun.

Bringing the barrel to their lips, he waited until the creeping blood passed the barrier of his lips, and when he tasted it finally, he squeezed the trigger.

Torrence pulled back quickly, letting the bullet ripple through the vibrating air between them, eventually reaching the blood that was rushing from her lips and crawling into Wesley's. It pushed the gelling liquid in all directions, creating a circular burst of spilling blood in the air.

She looked to it in anticipation, licking the blood from her lip and chin and drawing it back into her mouth. As she swallowed it, she raised a hand to blood in the air. It shook, held its place, then shifted as she manipulated its slowed motions with her speedy ones into the snake and the horns and she drew six of the seven points.

"Yes," she exhaled, her shoulders falling in relief. Arrogance passing through her features. "Yes."

She quickly withdrew a second vial from her pocket and let the blood-symbol drip slowly into it as the bullet continued its path, however slowly.

At the precise second when the bullet hit the wall, time returned to its normal speed. The remnants of the floating symbol fell into the vial and ran down Torrence's hand.

Jason removed himself quickly from the woman, and he and Michael took off with Freddy out of the room.

"It worked?" Wesley asked, placing his hand on Torrence's shoulder. "I couldn't look fast enough to see."

"It worked," she said. "He was kindness."

Wrapping his arms around her, Wesley nestled his face into her neck. The scents of sweat and blood lingered on her skin, and he inhaled it deeply. It felt like power and violence, and while she had other followers, none were invited to actively participate in the ritual as Wesley was.

"Thank you for letting me be a part of this," he said. "I know you don't have to share the blood with me. I don't want you to think I don't appreciate that."

"Of course you appreciate it," Torrence said, the sound of a smoke detector ringing out in the distance.

"What does Conrad say?" he asked. "About doing the devil's work..."

"'Erase the purity of virtue,'" she quoted to him, "'Gain the power of sin.'"

CHAPTER THREE
The Communion

Torrence stared out the windshield.

"So," Wesley said, looking over to Torrence. "How's that supernatural astigmatism tonight?"

Large crosses of glowing fog beamed out of each street light, each headlight of each passing car. Every green light omitted X's of their hazy color far into the sky, and when the car stopped at red lights, the crimson beams of the cross-like lights seemed to invert in the night air— a beacon of darkness rising against the open sky.

"Miraculous," she said.

"What does it look like when it storms?" Wesley asked.

"The lightning bolts," Torrence said, pulling on the seat adjuster to lie back and gaze into the starry night through the moonroof. "Each jagged line expands into four more lines. All light. All blurred. The rips in the sky, the tears in the atmosphere, they branch out too. Everything is bright and blurry. Everything blends into everything else, and nothing feels a separate entity from anything." She looked over to him. Gleaming light reflected against his irises, creating bursts of light inside his eyes. Torrence lifted her hand. Watched the lights of passing buildings and street lamps bounce off of her flesh, then she looked to his hand. She reached for it. Held it. Watch the light beams blend his skin into her skin, and for a moment, she felt nothing of him and everything of him all at once. They were connected, but not as two separate forces which were feeling one another. Now they just were. They existed. They were matter and energy and space and time. They were souls, spiritual beings, but each a piece of the same eternal matter. They were not bodies or brains or even personalities. They simply were. "You feel like a part of me. Maybe I'm a part of you."

He liked that, this idea that he and Torrence might be one. One being, one spirit, one soul, one body; he didn't care. Just the thought— that intangible, indescribable flicker of the mind— sent his heart into a rush of pulsating emotion, which colored the skin across his high cheekbones with warm hues of pink.

He wished he could see the world through her eyes, her after-communion eyes— not because he wanted the blood or the power or the hazy light beams, but because he yearned to look at his hand against Torrence and see his flesh melt into hers.

Maybe in the cemetery, maybe the night when all seven communions have completed. Only two more now.

"We're here," Wesley said, but his voice barely registered. Torrence didn't even notice the car stopping. She didn't notice the stillness of the world outside her window.

Lost inside her eyes, staring at the parted sky, Torrence felt the buried blood calling to her. All five vials shook inside the earth when she drew near, the fresh communion still pulsating inside her— blood called to blood; pulled her body towards the mausoleum, shifted the earth above the buried vials.

It tingled, the blood in her veins. She liked to make it wait, liked to feel the static tickling her beneath the flesh.

"Torrence," Wesley said, opening the door.

Her head drew back into the rest, turning, running the skin of her cheek along the velvety fabric wrapped around it. A small chuckle came.

"Tor," Wesley said, trying to gain her attention.

She focused only on the call of the blood, on the need of the communion in her body to join the offerings in the ground.

Her feet twitched, then like a rising tide of vibration, the static moved up her calf, her thigh until her legs were shaking. The muscles in her stomach tightened. Her hands reached out for anything, gripping respectively the emergency brake on her left and the seatbelt on her right. Her eyes tightened and she laughed. Sick, maniacal, painful pulls of breath left her smiling lips in a litany of growl-like cackles.

35

"Torrence, stop!" Wesley grabbed her shoulders. "Come on," he urged, tugging at her.

Her head remained on the rest, her shaking legs planted firmly against the seat. Only her shoulders drew nearer to the outside when he urged them from the car.

"Torrence!" he yelled, releasing her, and when her back touched the seat again, her lips closed.

All at once the shaking stopped, and her eyes opened.

Gleaming like the waters of a deep, endless pool of blood, Torrence's pupils blew wide and overtook her irises and the sclera of each eye.

Though this was the fifth time Wesley had seen her eyes in this mystic state, he recoiled at the initial sight of them. It didn't become ordinary, even though it was now customary. It was expected, but still jarring. Uneasy in its usual manner.

Torrence's vision was overtaken. She saw only blue-blacks and maroons, and outlines of shapes significant-enough in size to bleed through the veil.

Looking at Wesley, she marveled for a long moment over the outline of his body, the colors surrounding him, the golden hue at his head and the deep browns around his hands.

"Are you an angel?" Torrence whispered, a long fingernail finding its way to her teeth and teasingly playing with her lips there. "No," she purred. "Maybe a demon."

"Torr," Wesley breathed lowly, his voice shaking in his throat. "Come on." He swallowed thickly the nerves and worry and fear which formed an unpleasant ball, a ball which pushed at his vocal chords and expanded each time he tried to speak. "We gotta... We gotta get you—"

"Yes," she said, smirking. Her hand floated away from her lips and unfurled in the air to offer him her palm. "Escort me, little brother. Will you?"

"Yes, ma'am," he said, taking her hand and helping her from the car as she feigned this arrogant, classic demure— a sick depiction, this caricature of femininity in the height of 1922 fashion, or some other classically appealing visage, he thought. But what lurked inside was something monstrous hidden beneath the creamy flesh and silken hair.

The way her toes pointed when her leg flowed from the car, the way her body turned in one fluid motion when her other leg lifted to join it, her straight back as she stood, the hand delicately resting on his— oh, here at the cemetery gates, draped in the darkness of the hour, Wesley imagined her in a tight, black dress with a layered pearl necklace gleaming in between lengthy finger-waved curls.

Elegant she became under the influence of the blood. Easy, smooth. It wasn't the cool, sharp Torrence of murder and violence. It was something different. It was authority and dominance, but it wasn't aggression. Still, as appealing as it was, it was terrifying.

"Don't be scared," Torrence said gently, patting Wesley's hand with her free one.

He looked over to her, his movements quickened by the unnerving suspicion that, in this state, she could read his mind, and, oh, what tragedy might befall them, their brethren-gang, if she heard all that bounced around his brain, fueled by emotion and want instead of hate and violent delight.

"You're shaking," she said, but she smirked and a brow raised over one of those deeply-crimson eyes.

"It's cold," he lied. Turning back to face the path ahead of them, Wesley shuddered. He was her eyes. He couldn't risk looking at her for too long, not in the dark, not this late at night.

Besides that matter, Wesley was never really sure if it was Torrence he was seeing when he looked at her in these after-communion hours, not when they drew so near to the buried blood.

The calmness that entered her body with it, that ease that made even the most devilish smirk seem a sincere smile, it felt otherworldly. Demonic.

He supposed it was. But then, did that mean it wasn't her?

Power, after all, was what she sought, and he supposed the mystic charge of sacrificial blood might provide that. He wondered why she wanted it before they found Conrad, why she didn't seek him out first and follow him through his own rituals.

It wasn't like Torrence to be a follower, but devout to her satanic savior she was indeed.

"Oh," she said, interrupting his musings. "I can see the sacraments." She whined something delicate and enjoyable. "I feel them."

"Yes," Wesley said. "A few more feet."

Even though he always offered to dig, Torrence insisted she do it.

Refusing to use a shovel, she wrapped fists around the grass and dug it up, tossing it aside or behind them; it didn't matter.

Blinded to anything earthly, her blood-red eyes instructed her hands in the dirt. She pulled up handfuls. Bent knees in the dirt. Dirt under fingernails. Blood-stained knuckles covered in soil, bugs scattered away from her, hurrying away from whatever she emitted in these manic moments of instinct and inspired-act.

When she finished, Wesley marveled. Each time the hole was perfectly round, the exact-right distance from the other offerings. This one— the one he believed to be the fifth— formed the final point of the top shape where two triangles interconnected. A Star of David of sorts, which seemed opposite to their devotions, but then, wasn't that the point?

Wasn't all the savior said, wasn't all that appealed so deeply to Torrence within him, a pursuit of inverted faith?

Oh, what might they feel or witness or experience if they stood before Conrad only to discover that he was, in fact, the anti-Christ? What he might be able to do if he truly was the son of evil, and not just a demonic blithe upon the world.

Since the tape's surfacing, that was the belief held by his devotees— that he was possessed but not taken-over. He wasn't controlled. Wasn't ridden. He wasn't merely a vessel, but something more. A soul blended with a fallen angel, the deviance was the demon attaching itself to his brain, confirming to him that every sick depravity he wanted to enact was not only possible, but entirely justified; he was something unique. He was allowed this violent act and that one. He could do them because he was Conrad, because he was chosen, because the possession did not overtake him, but instead empowered him.

Wesley wondered if Torrence was simply empowered, or if they were playing fire; with the forces of fire and brimstone. Did she truly know what she was getting them into? He didn't, but he went along with it all the same. He supposed it was something about her that enticed him to it. Something about their petty thefts and run-of-the-mill muggings that filled his pre-opened-sky memories with the warmth and fondness one felt when remembering time shared with their favorite person.

He supposed Conrad was Torrence's favorite person, but of all those she knew, of all those she controlled, Wesley was comforted in the thought that he might be her favorite of the lot. At least until thoughts of their should've-been-second victim bubbled up from the vile spots of his subconscious.

It didn't matter that she saw this man, this strangely mild man, and suddenly decided he would not be the perfect specimen to provide the cure to chastity.

It didn't matter that she decided, for the first time in their ritualistic killings, to spare a life from damnation.

It didn't matter, Wesley told himself, because she hadn't done it for the man's sharp jawline or his taut, little frame. No. She hadn't done it for his glittering hair and crystal eyes. Wesley was certain, he argued with himself as he watched her here in the cemetery dirt, that she'd seen, with her demonic, communion-fueled, mystic sight, some sin within the would-be sacrifice that rendered his blood useless.

As a matter of fact, he further persuaded himself, Torrence's abilities grew so much with each communion that he was certain she could perceive things no one else could— except maybe those demons and the angels who were supposedly falling from the open sky, but wasn't that logical?

Wouldn't blood sacrifice give her the sight of demons, and wouldn't demons, who were simply demented angels deformed by their deviance, have the sight of angels?

Yes, Wesley told himself, that man was merely a mistaken saint. Wesley was her favorite, he was sure. But only so long as they were apart from Conrad.

Wesley wondered if Torrence wanted strength to save herself, and hopefully him, from the savior's wrath if he found them unworthy of his flock. Surely they were more than qualified, more than devoted, but to whom? And why?

"One more," Torrence said.

"One more?" Wesley asked, confused. "You mean two?"

"Oh, God," she exhaled. "Fuck."

"It's okay," Wesley knelt down beside her. He placed a hand on her back, a gentle touch, loving and protective.

"Oh, God," she said again, her lips curling in the agony of rising blood. Her throat burned as the sacrament rose. She covered the vial with her hands, bringing them together at the first fingers and thumbs to form yet another triangle, then brought her forehead to them. Closed her supernaturally-charged eyes, and let the blood spill from her lips. It gushed from her nose, dripped from her ears. She cried crimson tears of the unholy communion.

Wesley stroked her back. Pulled her hair away. Sat by and allowed her the expulsion. His own, merely a few droplets of the shared blood pooling at the corners of his mouth.

It burned when it touched his flesh. Its rise, something like a strong bout of acid reflux. He couldn't image how badly the swallowed-blood must've hurt Torrence when the tiny bit given to him from her deadly kisses felt like fire on his lips, but at least it was confirmation that it worked; that it worked for both of them. Whatever Torrence had planned, she worked Wesley into her goal too.

It comforted him, this acknowledgment, as he comforted her. He rubbed her shoulders gently. Let his hand fall comfortingly on her spine. He whispered and cooed, and felt not as her inferior or follower, but in these moments of physical weakness, of supernatural sickness, as her equal. A partner, perhaps.

After what always felt like an eternity, Torrence screwed her eyes shut tightly. The mysticism drained from them, they merely tingled, itched. She reached a muddy hand up and rubbed at them.

"Here," Wesley whispered, pulling a handkerchief from the inside pocket on his hunter-green jacket.

"Thanks," Torrence said. Her hand gently gliding through the air which was now recognizable to her human flesh as chilly. Slightly cold now that the heat of hell fled her body.

Her fingers connected to the silken fabric. She pressed it between her fingers, felt the delicacy, the softness of the silk, then she let them flutter away from it. She touched Wesley's fingers where they held it, the back of his hand, his wrist.

With this silent permission, Wesley moved the cloth against her face, her hand still wrapped around his wrist, and he wiped the dark, iron tears from her eyes.

Her lungs filled harshly. Released the same. She breathed at this pace for a long moment, and then her eyes opened. She blinked incessantly for a time, her vision blurring still then focusing, her eyes itching here and there and tingling in the after effects of the special sight.

"You okay?" Wesley smiled worriedly.

"Good," she said, returning the gesture. "You?"

"Good," he said.

She smirked. Her tongue ran over her teeth. "Good," she said, her voice low and quiet, but containing all the intensity of a scream.

Torrence lunged at Wesley, her body toppling his into the dirt. She pinned him down, nails digging into the flesh of his wrists, and, glistening in the moonlight above the graveyard in which they laid, she leaned down over him and bit at the tender skin of his neck hungrily.

Wesley exhaled breathily. He moaned beneath her, her power, the violence. He tried to push his wrists up, tried to shake them free of her grasp. His efforts, though they tired him, did little to her. The motions of his writhing body beneath hers registered as mere trembles to her, in her force, in the strength of her spirit which manifested itself now within the cells of her physical being.

Wesley chuckled. His eyelids fluttering closed at the sensations, at the biting and the kissing and the connection of Torrence's body with his own. What fun it was to be helpless, overpowered, and controlled; how safe it felt to find comfort in the arms of another person, to be taken care of, and protected.

In his desire to be taken, he thrust his hips upward as much as he could, signaling to her that he was not only consenting to be used in this way, but that he was eager for it.

Take me, Torrence, he thought as she tore at his jeans more like a ravenous animal than a human with thumbs and delicate fingers capable of unzipping and unbuttoning and easing fabric downward. Oh, Torrence, yes, God, my God, my God, here and now and in the flesh, yes, take me, and make all of the night's violence yours.

They didn't have to be in the cemetery to congregate in such a way. It didn't have to be dark around them, still inside the early morning hours where only the dead surrounded them and the living slept as if they were the dead. They didn't have to be high on adrenaline from a robbery or arson. The communion blood didn't need to be within him or expelled from them into the ground for such togetherness. But it always felt different to Wesley when it was.

For a moment, Torrence's body was weakened and he could feel like she needed him, that he wasn't just a sidekick or a driver or an underling with one of the few handguns left in the new, open-skied world. Then immediately after serving some grand purpose of physical comfort, he provided release in the same fashion. He was the warmth of living flesh after a night of death, he was one of two necessary pieces in the act of creation after an evening of destruction, and here, surrounded by the inevitable decay of rotting skin clinging onto to skulls and skeletons, he was the breathy moan of working lungs and the rhythmic heartbeat of physical exertion; he was necessary in these moments of desire and passion, and because it was called the 'sin' of the flesh and not the 'virtue' of it, he felt assured in her assertions that God is not good and that the devil merely wanted humanity to enjoy being alive.

It was good here in this sin of the flesh and Torrence, with her eyes of tingling, supernatural astigmatism and her bloody knuckles and her nails filled with dirt, well, Torrence was his leader and his friend and his confidant and his master.

Follow her to the ends of the earth, he would. But in the moments after the haze of lust and the blur of loving her cleared, after they'd felt ecstasy in the pleasures of the other, when their bodies were back inside their clothes and they were sitting again in his car, he wondered why she didn't want to go back to his apartment with him and sleep inside the cradle of his arms in the comfort of his bed.

He drove the car cautiously when they headed back to her place. Slowly, for he wanted to question this aloud, but couldn't muster the strength it might take to say something which could potentially lead to the disintegration of whatever it was they had.

A simple "good night" exchanged between them, a kiss on his forehead, and the car door shut. She never looked back when she walked away, not since the night of the mistaken offering, and Wesley tried not to imagine why.

Though Wesley was aware of War to this extent, War was not aware of him at all. War simply knew when Torrence re-entered the home. He felt her presence as it drew nearer to him, and when she came back into the bedroom, he wondered why she went straight into the shower when she was so obviously drained of energy and in desperate need of sleep.

He laid silently waiting for the water to stop running. He always let her slip back into the room, and crawl into the bed before he moved or spoke.

His arms came around her, and their bodies curled into each other's, and the warmth of War filled Torrence with a light, easiness formed only by gentle connection and soft breath; a sensation of tranquility and trust that no person had ever been able to provide. Something easy and calm. Something delicate, soft, but smooth, and free from the confines of guilt, or trauma, the pain of past experiences, the worry of the future; it was free from the heavy weight of sin.

Typically War kissed her shoulder. Most nights he wished her sweet dreams. But tonight, as he curled his arms around her, he buried his face into the crook of her neck and felt thin lines of broken flesh there. Four of them. Scratches.

"Where..." he whispered, but he paused. His brows tightened above his eyes and his lips closed briefly against her flesh. They didn't press against her, however. They didn't close at her skin to caress it delicately. They pouted. They closed tight in consideration, forming a straight line against her back instead of warm, almost-wet O around the smallest bit of it. "Where do you go?" War asked finally, nestling his forehead into her now, holding onto her tightly, as if she might escape his embrace and be lost to him forever.

"What?" She breathed, eyes fluttering around the wall as if she'd find whatever answer he sought scribbled across the paint there.

"When you leave at night," War said, "where do you go?"

She swallowed as she considered it— the nights and her activities and her companions— and compared the sheer force and aggression of the desires that compounded within her brain to create the essence of her soul to the gentle purity of War and everything about him that seemed too good to be human broadly and man specifically. "Nowhere you'd be interested in," she said. "That's why I don't invite you."

"I do not think I would accept an invitation," he said, biting at his lip as he considered it. "One must take care, Torrence," he whispered, lifting his hand to the jagged lines on her back and letting his fingertips follow the paths of Wesley's nails, "not necessarily of where one is invited," he continued, watching her skin heal beneath his touch, "but of what one invites into themselves."

Finally, where her flesh was whole again, he pressed his lips against her.

CHAPTER FOUR
The Cure for Chastity

War always walked home from Torrence's house. He knew it was a simple pleasure but he walked everywhere he could. Sure, it wasn't as fast as the usual method, and it required more effort, but it felt genuinely liberating to him.

It was just his legs, his feet. His body standing upright and moving. No reliance on anything but him; the strength of his physical form and the ability of his spirit within to command it to move.

Humans never seemed fascinated by these types of strengths, these simple tasks like walking or sitting upright or gripping an item with the opposable thumb and forefinger and holding it, let it alone the remarkable creations these appendages allowed— the gripping of a smooth hunk of wood and directing its attached bristles on canvas to design visual art, or the swift motions of fingers pressing string against wood to create the audible melody of music, or the pushing of keys on typewriters then later on keyboards to form words into sentences into paragraphs into books.

And language, oh, human language. The ability to grunt and wail and twist tongues and teeth and lips together to form words; words that became labels for objects— like chair, for example, but a chair wasn't a chair, it simply was, and humans assigned it certain sounds to communicate to one another what item they were describing when they said 'chair.' And beyond labels, words grew into sounds like 'fear' to describe an unseen sensation, and formed words like 'soul' and 'heaven' and 'hell' to represent, not a physical item or an assigned emotion, but entire concepts. Wow.

War was fascinated by this, this language, these languages, these words. He thought of words like 'Torrence,' words that represented people, individuals, and he was momentarily proud of himself for his choice of name. His name, which had been carefully considered, represented a great artist he'd grown to love upon immediate witness to his soul turned into tangible, consumable art.

Oh, art. He grimaced here in the street, in the purple haze of five a.m. He'd almost forgotten that art had been his task here, not Torrence, not language, not the broken skies, and not the end of the world.

Exhaling through his lips, War paused. His feet stopped moving. He merely stood there on the concrete of the sidewalk, this functional work of art that humans never seemed to notice, not as carefully as they could've considered it anyway, and he stared at the sky. Gazing into the vaguely perceptible colors of the heavens— the yellow glow of the sun kissing the amethyst skies of nighttime, creating beautifully orange-toned pinks that seemed as much light as it was dark— he considered praying.

Hesitantly he closed his eyes, fearful of what answers he might receive, equally as fearful that he might not receive any, and he shut his lips tightly and let the used-up air flee his nostrils in a very sharp, very human expression of his internal dilemma.

"Our Father..." he whispered, and against the black screen of his eyelids flickered an image of Torrence. It stopped him.

He could not pray with such images in his mind— images of human beauty and love, yes, in this way the face of Torrence in his thoughts was reverent. It praised the glory of God in this humanity, His greatest creation, but within that reverence and love grew desire and sinful want of skin-to-skin contact. War frowned; he shouldn't even have skin.

His brows creased over his eyes, his eyes which were closing more tightly now. He thought for a moment he'd injured them, but the sensation, burning and uncomfortable, he discovered to simply be tears. Sorrow. Regret. Sadness. Guilt. And that dreadful desire still urging him onward, suggesting that these horrid emotions were not valid, and what blasphemy it was to even entertain those suggestions.

Oh, War could not have fathomed these emotions or these desires some time ago. His entire existence had been void of them. It was meant to be that way, yet here he was standing on the earthy plane in an earthly body which urged him toward endeavors no one of his cosmic make-up was meant to experience.

But how glorious Torrence had been inside that museum. When the retina of War's eyes received the low lights of the Arctic Room illuminating her figure, the visual recognition sent straight to his brain read simply: beautiful.

He knew he shouldn't speak to her. They were not supposed to speak to anyone unless they had to, and there had been no pressing matter which required it. Still, the urge to say hello to her and hear the sound of her voice in return was undeniable.

But War was strong of spirit and very devout, and these were two of the main reasons he'd been chosen for this mission.

After the fall of the Watchers those millennia ago, all had been called back behind the front. Gates were locked. No flesh or spirit trapped on one side or the other could break or pass through.

This was different, though. This was not the time of life and beginnings. This was the time of death and endings. This was the time of the parting skies, and when the sky opened so too did heaven open.

Though War had never visited a museum until those the months before the sky opened, he had seen images of artwork, of sculpture, of the bindings of books, and the mechanics of bass drums. All in his legion had access to these things, which was why his particular mission, this research of art and discovery of soul through it, seemed rather odd at first.

Once he stepped foot inside the first museum, however, he'd understood it. Art in person was nothing like art through a screen, and he suddenly understood why modern people still preferred paperback books to online copies and why concerts were explosions of life even to those who owned their own private copies of the music.

No, seeing the paintings from afar was nothing like standing before them, witnessing the various colors of product like tiny cells of human DNA and imagining each separate stroke of paint as blood vessels and muscle tissue and brain matter.

War had wanted to touch these pieces but he knew that this was not allowed. A human rule placed on human creations much like God's rule placed on his favorite creatures.

46

No, War, the humans do not like you to touch the paint and God does not like you to touch the humans.

But he was allowed to look at the artwork of man so looking at the artwork of God must have been all right too. After all, whose artwork War was meant to research had never been specified. He was simply told he'd know the soul when he sees it.

War thought it had been the soul who spoke to him immediately, the soul he'd named himself after, the soul of pop art and soup cans and glorious portraits of the celebrities humans viewed as sub-gods. Marvelous.

But War hadn't been recalled, so perhaps it wasn't this soul. Either way, War didn't think there was a painting or a poem in existence that matched the artistry of this woman— her small frame, shapely figure, high cheekbones, creamy flesh. The simple pearl necklace she wore— natural, he could sense that— and elegant; paired with a diamond necklace that laid gently at the base of her neck. Her long hair flowing like a river of onyx made even the worn, leather jacket on her shoulders appear resplendent.

Opulence seemed to hang in the air around her, but War supposed it could've just been the lighting. Even still, he'd seen plenty of women and plenty of men pass under these same lights, and many like them in similar museums, and he'd never seen a face so striking that it made the glitter of heated lamps appear so trivial that it registered to the eye as mere adornments on its skin.

The walls around her, the other people in the room, the sharp contours and bright colors of paintings all faded into gently flowing blurs around her— this woman across the room from him; this elegant creature, this muse of the poets, goddess to the savage men around her, siren to the forlorn sailor.

Finally, after a long moment of voyeurism, acknowledgment came.

Torrence's bright blue eyes flickered in his direction, met with him and his face and his eyes on her, and he looked away hurriedly.

Yes, his eyes devoured as much of the hues of her eyes as he'd allowed them, and, yes, they begged him for more. They shifted quickly back and forth between her and the painting he'd been studying, vibrating in their confusion to the point that War had to shut them and place his fingers against their lids.

Cursing himself briefly, War turned his body away from Torrence, ashamed and embarrassed. What sensations flowed through him now. Sensations! Oh, he felt like a Watcher, a biblical creature so enamored by the fairness of a daughter of Adam that they'd traded immortality for a chance to copulate with them.

Fallen angels. Damned souls.

War didn't want to fall. He didn't want to be damned. So he ran.

As he walked the streets now, War scolded himself. He couldn't feign ignorance or excuse himself, for he knew the moment he'd seen Torrence that her beauty was tempting.

Could he be forgiven now? Did it matter?

When he exited the museum that night, he decided to leave paintings alone for a few days, to forget statues and pop art and Picasso.

He stood on the street for a brief moment, looking around this time for a museum of books— libraries, they were called— and when he discovered one, he wondered if there might be a museum dedicated to music and song.

Perhaps inside a song of metal music or a work of gothic literature there would be a sign of this soul. All art was human spirit, and War wondered if this woman and her appealing personage hadn't been God's way of redirection. Leave the visual arts, War. It is audible or hallucinatory, this soul. Seek it out.

But it was to no avail. When he heard rock music, he felt the incomparable desires of love ballads and beauty. Briefly in the record store, he thought he caught a glimpse of the elegant, black hair and glistening diamond chain from the corner of his eye. He was obsessing.

It didn't help that he saw the woman's face in his mind's eye and considered what it might be like to know her and love her the way Jon Bon Jovi loved the subject of his song titled "Always."

Within that song, Romeo and Juliet was referenced, so War attempted to read the classic play, to consume literary art next, but the concept of lovers forbidden from expression of their love seemed nearer to War than it should have.

Instead he settled on a horror piece created some 1,800 years after the birth of Christ, assuming nothing personal could be found within it, and what a blasphemous idea that he should even have the ability to feel something personally, and weren't all of these thoughts and emotions brought on by the mere sight of Torrence the reason he was here in this library reading fiction?

Yes, better to read about impossibilities. To remind himself that what he was becoming was an impossibility. But as he read the work of Mary Shelley, he related very much to her Modern Prometheus who cursed his creator for bringing him to this earth and then abandoning him.

War shook his head. Tried to focus on the words on the page, not on the ideas of what they might mean to him, but the fact that this book contained monsters, or beings called monsters by man, could not have been accidental.

Divine intervention perhaps guided his human hands to its spine— to the spine of Shakespeare before it, and to the records of eighties glamour gods— and maybe God wanted him to see that woman, but why? He tried to justify it; Maybe God didn't mind desire. Maybe War was meant to feel emotions simply to better understand them, maybe he just wasn't meant to act on it.

He decided to go back to the museum where he'd seen her. He could look at her, watch her. He could hear her voice, and none of that was sin, was it?

Or maybe this was mere justification for an act he knew to be wrong. He wasn't sure then, and he wasn't sure now.

When War walked home, he paused when the wind blew. He let himself experience its refreshing chill as it caressed his face. Feelings weren't always spiritual, were they? And if God gave him physical sensations then surely it was God who had given him these new spiritual sensations too.

No, he shook his head. Continued his pace. It was blasphemy just to imagine.

Perhaps he wasn't strong enough to resist such a temptation. Maybe this was a test. Looking into the sky, War acknowledged this, this weakness of his spirit, and he assured the heavens that he would not falter. He would do his job and that alone. But he wasn't certain his convictions were more than hopeful lies.

He wondered if God believed him.

He climbed the stairwell in silent reflection. Why were material concepts so appealing? The skin of a beautiful woman, the taste of a glass of Chardonnay. These things weren't evil, but it was man's desire for them— Humanity's desire for them. Desire that festered in an individual's insecurity and powerlessness, festered until it became less about the object of desire and more about the act of choice. Choose to sin. Choose to treat the temple as a bar or a brothel. Choice. How many humans turned away from God simply because He instructed them to choose His path over any other.

And the other himself— the Adversary. How fun his code of conduct must've seemed to someone who spent their entire life sheltered away from it. After all, wasn't Lucifer simply an angel who wanted to sip wine and sing with humans? Didn't he simply see a chance for choice when the warriors of God were never given such a superpower as free will?

War understood now more than ever that first fallen angel. He felt dirty for it, for seeing a human being and desiring knowledge of her, her mind, her soul, the closeness only two spirits could share because they had the choice to.

But he was disturbed by yet another thought— the thought that these desires came from that dark ruler himself, the dark ruler who witnessed all as God witnessed all, and who was determined to corrupt as many of God's virtues as he possibly could.

War did not want to be weak. He did not want to be a victim to the most beautiful, most vile angel in existence.

But he wanted to see the woman again. Wanted to know her name, that's all. Just a name. What harm could there have been in that?

He decided, as he approached his apartment door that night, that he would return to the art museums and to the paintings of his beloved Andy Warhol and that, if he saw this woman again, he would offer a smile when their eyes met. He would not run.

He prayed to God for a sign if this was wrong. Prayed for intervention, for guidance, for some hint as to who this soul was, as to what he was truly doing there.

His answer came as he stepped over the threshold of his door, for tangible hands were upon him, toppling him onto the linoleum of his kitchen, and bombarding him with the concentrated fury of the divine.

Every day since then, every morning he left Torrence's home, every morning like this morning, War stood before the bar beneath his apartment. Stared at the building. Always wondering what next retribution awaited him inside.

CHAPTER FIVE
Infestation

Torrence never minded waking up alone. Though she disagreed with War in most, if not all, matters, she understood him and his motivations. War did not leave her in the morning because he did not want to be with her. On the contrary, she knew War left because of how desperately he wanted her.

Everyone had a breaking point, no matter how devout, and if the fear of his own home did not push him entirely into her desires, then she was certain the final rip in the open skies and her position in the unholy hierarchy would cement his place, if only for his safety, by her side.

It seemed absurd to Torrence that her usual methods hadn't already obtained this particular desire, and had the final sacrifice not be set for a particular date, she would have pushed it off to prove that she could own War as she owned Wesley and the merry men of her gang without apocalyptic power. There was no choice, however, and no matter when the final virtue revealed itself to her, Torrence already knew its date of death. That date was drawing near. Not tonight, but soon enough.

Tonight would be a night of great preparation, of visiting her most trusted and ensuring all was ready for the final virtue, but before she could do that, she had one final task to perform. Today, she planned to return the tape, the divine prophecy itself. The beginning of the end before the end could have even been dreamt of.

The final virtue would reveal itself to her on her way there, she was certain of it. Its light would call out to her. Whether the body it dwelt within would be positioned near Torrence, perhaps in the car next to hers, or hidden safely inside its own home, it didn't matter. She'd consumed six sacrifices, each strengthening her, building her resistance to this pure light while also increasing its visibility to her.

Prior to Conrad, Torrence could have sniffed out sin. Now she could detect the sweet scent of morality from miles away. No one, not even the hoards who joined Conrad prior to Torrence could have done that. Even if they performed the rituals, it was not in their destiny to do so.

Many people had access to the prophecy and the prophet; to the teachings of Conrad and his very first tape. While they converted and followed and awaited that night of unholy providence, no one understood the message of that tape the way Torrence had. They simply were not destined to.

Torrence devoured the messages of the messianic figure. His memorandum had been watched and listened to and re-watched and repeated until it had been ingrained in her brain as deeply and as easily-accessible as the regulation of breathing inside its medulla oblongata, and this profound knowledge made the momentous date very obvious to her.

It was common knowledge that Conrad's favorite time of year was All Hallow's Eve, though he wreaked more havoc on the night traditionally meant for deviance. The night prior to Halloween: Devil's Night. For years he'd taken hoards of followers out to destroy and devastate on this date. He preached divine sermon, spoke of the days when disorder would be law and his flock would reign. He celebrated every year in chaos and destruction in honor of it. A High Holiday of the future, but now, in the time of open skies, thanks to Torrence, the future was here.

Torrence's mission this day, a vehicle to find that final virtue, yes, but a necessary method of expanding the congregation even one night before its leader took the throne.

Yes, returning the tape to the alleyway in which she'd been given it was beneficial to her goal, to everyone's goal, but she found it difficult to release the old video. She sat before the VCR she'd taken from Wesley's home, clinging to the tattered box as if the blood of her seventh virtue itself were housed inside it. She knew all that was said on it, all that was preached, and all that was prophesied, but was very early still, — War's guilt always awakened him before the sun rose, and Torrence rose shortly after— so there was time to enjoy the tape, full of static and sin, one more time.

Tears came to her eyes when it began. This was the last time she'd witness it, this start of not only Conrad's fate, but of hers, of the world they'd rule together now. Savior and Awakener. Seven sacrifices performed by each. The final rip before the sky burst completely, before hell opened up and demonic forces fled freely onto the earth. All would bow to the Savior, and to the Awakener who restored corrupt divinity to a fiendish god. She could not wait to find the virtue and to slit its throat.

As anticipated, virtuous light shone through the city. Unmatched by even the rising sun, its light beckoned Torrence's spirit toward it; a beacon of light illuminating the path to eternal darkness.

When she arrived at the motel, Torrence walked with the tape in her hand, ready to return it to Skeet, and ready to commit the final trespass against God.

It didn't matter that she'd already opened the sky. It didn't matter that she credited Conrad with that, or that she'd never met him. Not yet, anyway.

Soon that would change. This Devil's Night she'd join Skeet and Jack out in the wastelands beyond what remained of the inner-city because this Devil's Night she'd complete the seventh sacrifice.

"Boys," Torrence said, grinning as she entered the alleyway behind what used to be a twenty-dollar-an-hour hotel. Now that the sky had opened up, it was vacant, a rotting shell of shot-up plaster full of old needles and semen.

"Torrence." Skeet greeted her with a controlled excitement. "Wow," he said, "the end of the world has done you well."

"I never had any doubts," Jack said. "That blood's doing you good, isn't it?"

"You wouldn't even believe," she said. "I can sniff out a virtuous soul like a bloodhound, and their light barely even burns."

"Conrad will be happy to hear that," Skeet said, his grin ever-present in these open-sky moments with Torrence.

"Oh, yeah?" Torrence asked.

"Yeah."

"You're not gonna follow him," Jack said, chuckling. "Why do you act like you want to?"

"Conrad is the Savior, isn't he?" Torrence said stoically.

"You and Conrad," Skeet said. He slapped Jack. "The Devil and the Awakener."

"Whatever," Torrence said. "Here's the tape."

"You don't want to keep it?"

"I want it to spread," she said.

"Remember when we first found each other?" Skeet asked.

"I do."

"Me too."

"Me too," Jack said, grinning.

"I remember how violent you already were," Skeet said. "How beautiful and how violent." He eyed her. "But you paled in comparison to who you are now."

"Don't try to flatter me, boys," she said, running a hand through her hair. "I prefer you on your knees... In worship, of course."

"Of course," Skeet said, and in his eyes, Torrence saw the same man she'd met here so long ago. Just before the skies opened. Before she knew of Conrad or the salvation that was promised if only the right person, the Awakener, could give the rituals to the Messiah. The Unholy One.

The night she met her Boys, Torrence was dealing multiple products to multiple buyers.

Jocelyn had given her the last of her minuscule paycheck for some ketamine, and under the drug's influence, Torrence had convinced Jocelyn that sleeping with two men supposedly-named Bob and John was Jocelyn's greatest fantasy.

While Jocelyn enjoyed the effects of the ketamine, the men enjoyed Jocelyn, and Torrence stood outside the door of room 316 enjoying her cash.

In the silence of two a.m., even the scuffing of shoes could've been heard, but Torrence ignored the footsteps perceived. She kept her head down as they came closer, eyes on her money, and she extended out her arms further from her body and counted the cash more slowly, tempting anyone who might wander by to try and take it from her.

Two men approached. She could see them from the corner of her eye. When they paused before her, she grinned.

"Hi," the first one said. "I'm Skeet. This is Jack."

Looking up, Torrence locked eyes with one of them— a blond man with his hair parted in the center— then she glanced to the other who was also blond but spiked his hair in all directions.

Both men recoiled slightly when she gazed at them, something sinister perceived inside her no doubt; Torrence was far too accustomed to the discomfort in the face of someone whose instincts told them that her intentions were never good.

Elated by this, Torrence chuckled, but, oh, it had been so long since she'd last had a fight, a real tussle with someone challenging, and she exhaled her boredom as she looked back down to the fifties fluttering from one of her hands to the other.

She felt the men's eyes on her still; they were watching her hands, yes, but not for lust of the cash within them, no. Instead, they were studying the details of her fingers, the various cuts and scrapes scattered across her skin, the broken flesh of her knuckles, dried blood, scabs.

She was one to get her hands quite literally dirty, and she wore the evidence of that fact proudly.

The two men looked at each other. Torrence caught it. She moved her back away from the wall, jutting out her hip and straightening out her shoulders. She folded the bills at their center in one hand and tucked them away while her other hand ran through her raven locks. She laughed.

"Oh, boys," she said, stepping closer to them; her tongue swiping over the bright teeth behind her lips. "Do tell."

"We're not boys," Skeet said.

"You're whatever I tell you to be," she countered and the pair shared another look.

Skeet smirked sideways, fiendishly handsome and wasn't that his appeal? Maybe it was. Maybe it was something darker. Torrence always seemed to find the darkness inside of people, even before her eyes found their faces or their figures. A talent, she'd always supposed, a necessary talent for someone with her ambitions.

"Fine," he said. "Call us boys."

"What do you call yourselves?" She chuckled. "Men?"

"Followers," Jack said.

"Of what?"

"You mean who," Jack clarified.

Torrence snorted.

Skeet slapped him. "Mind your manners," he said to Jack, then looked back to Torrence. "Followers of the Savior," he said gently. Ravenous eyes devoured Torrence, slipping round her face and following her hair across her collarbones.

"That look's not one of chastity," she said.

"No," he clarified. "Not that savior."

"There are more than one?"

"There are two," he said, licking his smirking lips. "There's that one." His eyes rolled up toward the heavens, the blue sky darkening in the passing moments beyond eight p.m., and that had been so regular then. The sky had been so whole.

He looked back to her. Grinned something wolf-like, something hungry and vicious, but something very controlled. "And there's this one." From inside his leather coat came a VHS tape. Long fingers wrapped around this beaten-up box and strummed it when he raised it up between them.

"I'm not interested in your creepy uncle's porn collection," Torrence said, but she was very much intrigued by this tape. She hadn't seen tapes in years, not since she was a child or a teenager perhaps. What were these tattered delinquents doing with one now?

"I think you'd find this tape very interesting," Jack said.

"All right," she said, extending her hand for it. "I'll bite."

Another shared look. "Yes," Jack said. "I'm sure you would."

"You'll have to ignore him," Skeet said. "He's got no sense of subtlety."

"And what should he be subtle about, exactly?"

Skeet placed the tape in her hand. "The Savior," he whispered.

"And this Savior..." Torrence flipped the tape so she could see the back of the box. Empty and tattered, just as the front had been, the back revealed nothing about its contents, so she turned it and let the tape slip from its packaging. "He's on this, huh?"

"No," Skeet whispered, the soft tone painting his word with

astonishment and reverence. "No, what's on this tape is a teenager."

Torrence recoiled. "I don't do kids," she said, slamming the tape back into the box and tossing it back to Skeet.

"It's not pornography," Skeet said.

"Fine. I don't kill kids either. No kids, no animals."

"Do you mind if I ask why?"

"Because it isn't fun," she said simply. When Skeet's brow raised, she exhaled. "It's too easy. No fight physically or mentally. Anyone can manipulate a kid and even a kid can overpower a kitten. If hurting a kid or an animal makes you feel powerful, I feel bad. I mean, how tiny must your dick be?"

"So… You enjoy overpowering? Being dominant? In charge?"

"Maybe I enjoy it or maybe it's just how I am." Torrence shrugged. "Maybe I don't have a reason to do anything I like to do. Maybe I do but I don't yet know what it is. Either way this kid stuff—"

"No, you misunderstand," Skeet said, smiling. "The teenager here isn't hurt. He's being saved. At least, that's what his parents think, that's what the priest thinks."

"Priest?" Torrence looked back to the tape, eyes narrowing on it briefly. A dark grin overtook her delicate features. "What would a priest be doing on this tape?"

"An exorcism," Skeet said, that astonished tone returning, his eyes gleaming as if he were, himself, about to give a great sermon. "'And in exorcising the boy, the servant of the Lord God in Heaven released only its essence; leaving within the fragile body of flesh and blood all the knowledge of the demon.'"

"Are you trying to quote something Biblical to me?" Torrence scoffed. For as eerie as the man was, Torrence was well aware of the inaccuracy of his speech. "What passage is that from?" She smiled condescendingly. "I don't recognize it."

"Of course it isn't from the Bible," Skeet said. "It's from the tape. It's from the teenager when he was awoken; when he become something else, something more than a teenager, something more than a man or a person or soul."

"What did he become then?"

Skeet offered the tape again. "Watch. Listen. Let him awaken your purpose."

"Your true purpose," Jack added.

"My true purpose, huh?" She raised a brow but took the tape, unable to deny how very intrigued she was simply by the idea of watching an exorcism. How violent something like that must've been, not just for the body but for the mind and the soul.

"All of our purpose," Skeet said. "Hell on Earth. Angels will fall. The wicked will rise to ritual, slaying these angels through the righteous ones, killing their virtues and restoring glory to the correct God."

"The Messiah," Jack said, arching a brow as he stared at Torrence. "Our Messiah."

"Right, of course," Torrence said. "All right. I'll give it a watch." The sound of a door opened behind them. Men's voices cackled and congratulated one another. "That's my cue, boys. Gotta clean up the merchandise for the next customer. You understand."

"Of course we do," Skeet said, the smirk on his lips spreading. "You can find us here any night. Whenever you're ready, we'll be waiting."

Torrence watched the men slip away again, around the corner and into the alley created by this hotel and a dive-bar next door.

"Come again, gentlemen," she said as supposedly-Bob and supposedly-John bid her thanks and farewell. Then she peered into the room to ensure Jocelyn was still alive and well-enough. "Hey, J," Torrence said, unfurling a few of the fifties and throwing them on the small table beside the door. "If Ava comes by, just give her this for the night."

"Thanks, Tor," Jocelyn said lazily as Torrence closed the door.

She wanted to watch this tape immediately. Always drawn to the concept of evil, of wrongdoing and violence, Torrence made her way to her car.

She needed Wesley, his bedroom, the old technology he collected. She needed his VCR.

"One of my brothers lost their phone over this." Torrence chuckled as she handed it back. "I warned him not to try to record it."

"'Only those worthy to hear the word will work hard enough to hear it'," Skeet said. "It's not like phones do much these days anyway."

"Not now," Torrence said, her chin lifting in arrogance. "You're welcome, by the way."

"Thank you," Skeet said. "I'm not sure if you could hear me or not, but this isn't the first time I've shown you appreciation."

"One more ritual," Torrence said. "Then who knows what I'll be able to hear... or see... or do."

"You'll be able to do anything," Jack said, but he was met immediately by Skeet's silencing hand.

"Conrad really hopes to see you on the thirtieth."

"Tell Conrad I have plans tomorrow night. A celebration indeed. You see, this day is the twenty-ninth, but only until midnight."

"Three a.m.," Skeet said questioningly at first. Then he smiled. "Oh, three a.m. this night will be—"

"Three a.m. on the thirtieth," Jack said. "Wow."

"Do tell Conrad that he's more than welcome to come bear witness." Torrence grinned.

"Of course," Skeet said hurriedly, reverently. "Where should we tell him you'll be?"

Torrence leaned in, patting the tape in Skeet's hand. "Somewhere very close to home."

Skeet and Jack shared a look, then their eyes moved back to her.

"'And in the same solemn pit,'" Skeet quoted Conrad's voice from a recording called The Seventh Sin, wherein he murdered an overworked prosecutor in the name of sloth to forsake diligence.

"'Shall the final virtue be slain,'" Jack said, eyes widening, tearing up, as he fell to his knees.

Torrence patted his head gently. "'Against the wall which bears the solemn stains of the first virtue's corruption. The blood of the innocent melded with the damned shall never be washed away.'"

Skeet leaned down, placed a hand on Jack's shoulder. He looked up to Torrence, his brows rising over glassy eyes. So unusual the confident man looked with a slouch in his back, so odd to see anything but stern arrogance in his eyes. "You're really it," Skeet said, squeezing Jack's shoulder. "You're really the one Conrad has been waiting for."

"Weren't the open skies enough proof of that?" Torrence asked, but her tone was assertive. It wasn't a question she posed, but a test of faith.

"Of course," Jack sobbed, wiping at his eyes. "Of course, but we... couldn't predict whether or not you'd finish, whether you'd be stopped. An angel was said to—"

"To 'come down from the heavens when the first rip in the atmosphere allowed him passage', yes, I know. But no one is stopping me. I've been at this my entire life, long before Conrad could preach about me. The devil can't corrupt what was never good, and an angel can't save what's innately bad."

"Oh, Messiah!" Jack sobbed as he fell further onto the ground. "Our time has come! Unholiness will reign!"

Skeet swallowed thickly, watching his partner in praise and relief, and then he looked back to Torrence. "We'll tell Conrad," he said, his voice low and reverent. "The Savior and the Awakener shall meet at the inverse of the holy hour on Devil's Night."

"Good," Torrence said. "My brethren will be happy to serve their Savior when full power is restored."

Jack's body shifted as if to rise, but he was shaken and weak, and could only slightly move; the immense pressure of all belief-turned-reality still weighing heavily on his spirit, therefore taking a toll on his body.

Skeet reached for him, and their hands met, then he looked back to Torrence. "As will Conrad's."

CHAPTER SIX
Illumination

As she left the alleyway, Torrence struggled believing in a time before the sky opened. Even though it was a frightening concept to most, this end of times, it felt very natural to her. It was as if, for her and her brethren and her violent delights, the world should've always been this way.

Often times when Torrence considered the goodness that was so rampant in the time before Conrad and the rituals, she considered War. War, this devout Christian, this naive man in a cruel world.

She was never offended by waking alone after he stayed a night with her. She chalked it up to Catholic guilt. She imagined him slipping away, fearful of whatever sin he thought he'd committed merely by kissing her and touching her leg and falling asleep next to her, and she couldn't help but remember the first time she'd seen him and the first time she'd seen him up-close.

Torrence had felt powerful that night. She and Wesley and company were one virtue down— the first virtue taken— and she wanted more.

The Savior's voice played in her mind— the fearful tones of a young boy plagued by demons intermingling with the growls of the beast dwelling inside him. Oh, prophetic and foreboding was the message of the tape.

"What did he say?" Wesley had asked, out of breath and riddled with nerves as he stared down to the lifeless body at their feet.

Torrence grinned, the electricity of the ritual still blazing fire beneath her skin, and she recited the demonic spirit perfectly.

"And so the first virtue shall provide sight in its death so that the unholy may find more virtues to devour."

And, oh, Torrence had been given that sight. She imagined that's why she'd been so drawn to the museum that night. She remembered sensing an aura, a presence, something innocent and holy; purity within a body within a building within her very city.

She wanted that second victim. She could almost taste them, taste their blood. She hadn't expected one to present itself so soon, but she had committed the killing, consumed the communal blood and with it drew the serpent figure and the horns on its side and the first triangle in the seven points of sin. Time had slowed, proving not only that this ritual and these rites were real, but also that she was worthy of completing them. Yes, the sight had been given and she wasn't going to waste it.

She went straight into the building, never stopping at the desk to purchase tickets. Wesley followed closely behind her, tossing a couple of fifties onto the keyboard of the second employee's desk, accompanying Torrence while their brothers waited outside, each man appointed a different exit to guard.

Torrence wasn't sure who this virtue was, but she remembered Conrad and his possessing entity crying into the cement-box of a church's basement that when a bringer of sin became aware of the lights of virtue so too does virtue become aware of the presence of sin. All energy emits a light or a shade and spirits of the divine were easily recognized by one another, either by the illumination of the world around them or by the shadow cast across the land by their eternal darkness.

"I can't see anything," Wesley had said.

"And why would you?" Torrence answered, ascending the staircase to the fifth floor.

"The ritual—"

"You didn't take as much blood as I did." Torrence stopped, turned to look at him. "And you won't ever receive as much as I do."

"I wasn't questioning our hierarchy," Wesley said gently. "I just thought I'd see something."

"You see what I tell you to see," Torrence said, pausing just before the door of the sixth floor. Sparkling and glowing, the light trickling in from under the door, brightening even the dull concrete at their feet. "Shut up and wait here."

Wesley obeyed as always, but he watched Torrence through small, square window on the door.

She'd paused as soon as she entered the room, overwhelmed momentarily by the brightness of the virtuous aura. Oh, yes, it was here.

She moved slowly into the room, unable to glance around at the museum's patrons too closely, for the light was white-hot and burning brightly.

Torrence stared at the artwork on the walls instead. She moved toward the light instinctively, feeling its airy coolness upon her flesh and its intensity within her spirit.

It felt oddly good. It tingled as the communal blood had tingled, but this felt more the expression of power than the consumption of it.

She planned to change that. Conrad had made it very clear in the tape that each sacrament will bring more power so that the spiritual vision won't be as blinding or as painful to the physical body. Torrence was ready for it.

She rounded a corner, walked by a wall of large, silver Elvis Presley paintings. Glancing at the four individuals in the room, Torrence determined rather quickly that none were her target and pressed on.

Round another she followed the chill of the virtue. This time, when she entered a room guarded by porcelain sled dogs, she felt a distinct difference in the atmosphere, as if the human's sacrificial soul truly sensed her coming for it, and, in defense, turned the small section of the museum into an icy tundra.

She stared at the paintings on the wall— depictions of igloos and polar bears— marveling at the synchronicity of it all. Fate, surely, that the virtue hadn't been discovered by her demonic abilities in a room of floral springs or oceanic summers.

Regardless of her surroundings, Torrence knew she was in the correct room. The soul was here, the next virtue, and she quivered in the thrilling expectation of it.

Her eyes stayed on the wall until the hairs on her arms stood inside her coat. She felt her skin budding in the chill, tingling in the closeness, and under the influence of such intoxicating possibilities, Torrence turned her head away from the art.

Staring directly into the sun, Torrence thought briefly that she'd
seen blue eyes. What a marvelous pink-tone the flesh beneath them held.
Oh, yes, this body housed something miraculous, and in pursuit,
Torrence stepped nearer to it.

As slow as her pace was in both the blinding light and the frigid air,
the other's pace was quicker.

Hurriedly, the spirit fled, taking with it the illumination with which it
filled the space.

Cursing under her breath, Torrence chased the dimming light. It
moved so swiftly, however, that her earthly legs, fueled by the sacrifice of
only one communion, could not keep up with it.

She burst out of the museum doors to find Freddy and Jason.
Wesley came out just behind her, and Michael rounded the building until
he found them.

"Wow," Torrence said, more amazed at the powers of the blood
than disappointed at the loss of the virtue. Marveling, she whispered, "He
was so bright."

But that brightness made him easy to follow. His path illuminated by
his intention, Torrence directed Wesley to what seemed to be a bar.

"Some virtue," Wesley scoffed when they approached the
destination, but the intention of the virtue slipped around the building
and up a rusted staircase of black metal toward a large, faded-green door.

When her brethren grabbed War and threw him to the ground,
Torrence watched from the far end of the darkened apartment. No cries
came from him. No questions of who they were or why they'd come.

So odd this sacrifice from beginning to end, but she supposed they
had only experienced one prior, and the virtuous light which expanded
from his being as if he'd swallowed the moon could not have lied or
misled her.

Wesley first stepped away from the shuffle, his gun pointed directly
at War's human skull. Freddy followed him, using a hand to adjust his
fallen mask. Then Jason, then Michael.

War sat in confusion; he'd felt the wrath of God so plainly in the
hands upon him, in the swinging of arms and legs and in the connection
of fists and feet. Looking up to the figure nearest him on the right, War
saw only bright eyes above black fabric.

His brows tightened for, all at once, as swiftly as it had come, the fury ceased. He expected this man, this vehicle of God's punishment, to kick at him again or to strike him, something— he wasn't sure.

When nothing came, his eyes moved to the next figure, a stern-faced but very handsome man with lips in the shape of a beautiful bow. This man held a weapon in War's direction, and he took pause to consider how it might affect his earthly body if this man were to use it.

On his other side were two more figures, each yielding their own weapons though their stances made them seem less inclined to use them.

He looked down at his body, at his torn shirt and his pants riddled with dirt-imprints of boot-soles, and he lifted his hands to study them. He'd felt them burn when he was pulled to the ground; he must've fallen onto them. Wow. What a sensation. His nose hurt too, and so did his lips. He wondered briefly if he bled.

With the path cleared, the hoard in their rows of anticipation, Torrence came forward from the darkness of War's kitchen, which, in the open-floor plan of the tiny space, seemed very bright in her newly acquired spiritual sight.

As her boots clicked against his floor, War looked only at their composition. Wearable art as much as clothing was, and this consideration prompted him to look at her pants, her shirt, the jacket she wore, but he was so easily distracted by each tiny piece of each garment that it took him quite longer than it might've taken someone else to absorb her fashion choices.

By the time she bent down before him, trapped inside his glow with him, War hadn't yet looked up to her face. He'd become fascinated by a dangling charm around her neck. Small and silver, it appeared almost like a cross, but it wasn't one. It hung in shimmering glory beneath a single pearl and a thin strand of diamonds.

"It's a T," she said, blinking quickly, her eyes adjusting to the haze of light surrounding them. All-encompassing, Torrence thought for a moment that she could feel his virtue on her skin, caressing the tender flesh across her cheekbones. Gentle and soft and refreshingly cool, all could she think of when the man's face became clear inside his light was kissing him. "For..." she hesitated, her breath caught inside her throat by the visage before her. "Wow," she said, but this time it had nothing to do with the brightness of his soul. "You're beautiful."

"Beautiful," War said, his head tilting, brows creasing. "Is that why they've stopped?" His eyes pulled reluctantly away from the shimmering silver, landing on her face which stunned him. "Oh," he whispered gently, his features softening, looking warmly upon the leader of his attack. "You found me," he said in astonishment. "How did you find me?"

Torrence's brows raised in her own surprise. This man, glorious and virtuous, a physical representation of all she meant to destroy, was unimaginably perfect. Here inside his light, she could see him clearly. His cheekbones were high, jaw sharp, nose straight and small above subtle, pale-pink lips. An undertone of blue cast his creamy skin in a mystic, unearthly shade, and his hair, which had seemed blond from a distance, was quite iridescent where the light touched it.

"I followed your light here," Torrence said softly, almost cooing. Her sharp, violent features rearranged in his presence. She looked tranquil there inside his light with him, at ease and enamored.

"My light?" He responded in kind, gently even though he was excited.

"You emit the most wondrous light," she said, and War smiled, not for the seeming-compliment, but for his answered prayer— to hear the sound of her voice. "My brethren can't see it," she said. "You'll have to pardon them for their trespasses."

"'Forgive us our trespasses,'" he whispered. "I mean..." He sat up a bit, trying to become more present in the moments he shared with her, for he did not know how long their time would last. "Yes," he said. "Of course, they are forgiven. All those who seek salvation shall have it."

Torrence smiled, her lips more cunning now than they had been. "Salvation, yes." She glanced up to Wesley and nodded toward the door before looking back to War and his delicate beauty.

"But, Boss—" Wesley started, cut off by her release of a disapproving exhale. "Right," he said, eyeing the others. "Let's leave her to it."

Jason and Michael exited first, then Freddy. He held the door for Wesley, and when Wesley reached for it, Torrence addressed him again. "I'll meet you in the cemetery."

He paused, lips parting in confusion, but he said nothing. He obeyed Torrence and exited.

"A cemetery," War said. He hadn't considered the intricate artwork of tombstones or the wreaths woven in skill and compassion resting against them.

"Not to worry," Torrence said. "We just take a little something from every person we find, and we leave it there."

"As... an offering?"

"Yes." Thoughts of the vial buried beneath the dirt, the blood of the virtue they'd slain a mere evening prior. She grinned. "As an offering."

"What did you mean to take from me?" He asked delicately, still admiring her features, her radiant eyes, the shine of her hair.

A brow raised. Torrence glanced away from his gaze momentarily; the thought of lying to him, especially when looking directly into those eyes— eyes which not only gleamed so brightly in the dark, but were mesmerizing in their colors. Shards of plum and amethyst cut through seas of teal and blue.

In reaction to the chill his sight left on her skin, a physical reminder of the purity of the soul which shone through them and pressed itself against her, Torrence squirmed.

Though she wanted to stare at them, to watch the central point of black inside the flickering galaxies expand in seeking light, she couldn't. She blinked away. Studied the rest of the man, his face.

As her eyes moved down his nose and mouth, Torrence furrowed her brows. "You're not bleeding," she said, lifting hand to his face and brushing her thumb over his lower lip. "You're very pink in certain spots..." she leaned in more closely, eyeing imprints of knuckles and metal and boots. "Very pink," she said, popping her tongue against her teeth. "But your skin isn't broken anywhere."

"Oh," he said automatically, still in a haze. Then he came to understand what she had said. "Oh," he repeated solemnly, bringing his own hand to his face now. How odd this must have been for her, how odd he must seem to her now. But he rejoiced still; unlike the fallen Lucifer or his rebellious angels, God hadn't considered War as succumbing to his desires. Not yet anyway.

"You're so bright," Torrence whispered, petting his cheek, his eyebrow, his hair. "So bright."

But was just before the sky opened, back when a mere tear had been ripped. The first virtue taken in the name of darkness tore it ever so slightly.

The second, well, it would pull at the tear. It would stretch it, lengthen it. And with the third, a burst of lightning would open it with the flood of fire and thunder.

That was what Conrad had said anyway. That was what he predicted in his perfect-possession on the tape.

And War was still bright after all, but his virtue wasn't blinding, not anymore. Not after six sacrificial virtues. Each communion had increased Torrence's abilities, her strength. Purity no longer affected her the way it had when she first broke the seal between the ethereal and the earth.

She wondered, as she walked back to her car, what effect purity had on her now. After all, War had been a victim, so why was he in her bed instead of in the ground? Why was he slipping inside her veins in an effort to get to her heart instead in the aftermath of her communion?

He'd been beautiful, yes, but wasn't Wesley as beautiful? Wasn't Jason? She supposed it was that unnameable force certain people possessed— that appeal which couldn't be mastered or taught, which was only achievable by being born with it.

Her lips curled beneath flaring nostrils. That undeniable, indescribable allure, no, it couldn't have been purity. Goodness. At the thought alone, her throat burned with threatening bile. But the idea of goodness couldn't make her sick if the intimacy shared with its vessel didn't.

She turned on the car. Sat there for a moment. It was almost time for the final sacrifice. The seventh virtue had been made clear to her. A woman who worked behind the counter of a small Ma-and-Pop shop, a woman who volunteered at a soup kitchen and an animal shelter. A woman who donated ten percent of her meager wages to the church and another ten percent to a foundation which aided ill children.

This woman, she was charity, liberality, the cure for greed, and she was tagged for it.

Torrence would slay her in the darkness of impending night, surrounded by her band of brothers, with Conrad and Skeet and Jack present, and in so doing, Torrence would bring about the apocalypse.

What that meant for Conrad, for her demonic savior, well, everyone involved knew. Powers would be restored; the human cells would be awoken to their divinity and reanimated by the forces of the unholy. A birthright would be fulfilled.

But what did that mean for Torrence?

Torrence, as she pulled out onto the road now, ready to visit her most trusted follower, had always been in control of her own life. She did what she wanted when she wanted without compunction, and when she wanted company in her endeavors, she sought out the proper persons and convinced them to follow her.

It was strange, she considered as she drove now, how perfectly such things aligned; how she perfected her own individual crimes, how she had never been caught, not even for a petty theft or called out on pool-hustling, how she found her perfect follower then another then another, and how she found Skeet and Jack when she'd already gained their unconditional loyalty of those followers, and how Conrad's words seem to insert purpose perfectly into what she'd already been doing. The rituals, the victims, the sacrifices showing themselves so easily. The Awakener. The Messiah. The unholy union of these two human-beings in mutual deification. Wow.

Torrence hadn't only been a force to be reckoned with; she had been a force of fate and divine prophecy, and no matter how hellish that divinity was, divinity was divinity. Demons were mutated angels. The possessed were the enlightened. A murderer was the key to revival.

But as Torrence considered her dark savior's powers, she wasn't sure what she'd do when standing across from him. What would she say when she brought her comfort-weapon, her switchblade, to the neck of the final virtue? Would she say, "All this for you, my unholy lord!" because she wasn't certain that it all had been for him.

She loved him. She admired his power. She found beauty in both his flawless face and his deviant heart, but she did not want to be his follower or his friend or his partner. She wanted, if she were honest with herself, to be him. But there was no envy or ill-will toward him for his position; she did not want to be his enemy. She loved him.

At first she had been thrilled to find Conrad. His voice and his speeches and his crimes had been exciting and inspiring. The thought that she might be seated at the right hand of the devil when he took back power only she could take and twist and offer was validating; this life considered lesser by the general population of the world, this life of lawlessness and brutality, it was no longer a product of sadistic hedonism and sinful desire. Now, thanks to Conrad, her carnality, criminality, and chaos was kismet; her demonic destiny.

After a few rituals, however, the communions awoke within Torrence an ever greater strength. Physically and spiritually. She saw people more clearly— their virtuous lights visible from even miles away now— and when she wrapped a fist around their wrists, she no longer needed to press into pressure points to conquer them.

The power surging through her blended with the overwhelming ego already controlling most of Torrence's choices, and she stopped enjoying this second-in-command power position as much as she originally had, even when that meant heading an army of demonic beings and hoards of human followers.

She wondered how she might accept this Awakening position when what she had admired most in Conrad was his messianic status. Maybe, she considered as she pulled into Wesley's driveway, she never wanted to follow a savior, but to be one.

How disrespectful such a thought felt. After all, without Conrad and his orations and acts of disorder and destruction, she would not have the supernatural abilities she possessed now.

No one, not even the person who awakened the world to the apocalyptic anti-Christ, could turn their back on this divinely-charged deviant and survive. Even the Biblical lore of War's righteous and holy God said that.

As she approached the door to Wesley's house, Torrence reminded herself of his loyalty to her— of Michael's and Jason's and Freddy's— and she took comfort in the fact that while all they did was in service of the Savior, they worked toward that purpose because Torrence instructed them to.

If how they felt about her wasn't idolization, if what they were doing wasn't worship, then it was nothing.

Torrence tapped her knuckles against the door, and when Wesley opened it, she stared into his eyes.

Honey browns and caramels appeared golden in the sun's illumination.

Yes, Torrence thought as she sensed his soul behind those eyes, this is reverence; this is worship.

CHAPTER SEVEN
Descend the Rip

War approached the door to his apartment. He expected, as he had every night since Torrence, to be assaulted by some divine wrath, to be reminded of his abilities even now as he dwelt within human flesh.

Was God so angry with him that He had allowed War to be a victim of crime and deviance? He felt that had been true, but if it were, why wasn't he further victimized now?

He wanted to rationalize it, to claim that God was not disappointed in his closeness with Torrence, this lovely human woman, because his chastity remained intact even as he laid with her, but if this were true, that initial burst of vengeful violence shouldn't have to come to War at all.

The troubling side of this allowance of his actions, of the lack of punishment for his sins, was the idea that perhaps God was still angry with War, but so much so that now He had simply given up on him.

Dejected, and most likely abandoned by God, War inserted tiny, twisted metal into more metal, and unlocked his door. He felt his muscles tighten, which was becoming more and more commonplace for him as he opened his door and let the troubling thoughts of potential doom consume him. How strange that he had such thoughts— thoughts that stemmed from emotions like fear. Stranger still, his body reacted to these thoughts, these emotions. Was he becoming more human? Was that evidence in itself of his abandonment? Or would hands press upon him this morning, confirming both God's awareness of him, and His disapproval of his actions.

He inhaled deeply, trying to process so many new sensations and troubling thoughts, though he knew it was useless. There was no way War could master in ten months what humans spent their entire lives trying to conquer. It didn't matter, he decided. He'd have to accept whatever came upon him when he went inside, so he stepped over the threshold.

No hands assaulted him, though. No vehicle of punishment or correction was present upon him. No sign of God or divinity or forgiveness or wrath.

He flicked on the lights, however, and that changed immediately. War found his small home in shambles. As his eyes scanned the damage, he realized this wasn't an act of heavenly fury. This was simply a run-of-the-mill, end-of-days delinquency.

The two chairs in his humble kitchen were knocked onto the ground. The refrigerator door hung open, its contents— merely a half-drunk gallon of water and two jars of sweet pickles— had been opened and thrown about the space.

Perhaps the burglar had been seeking something in particular, War wasn't sure, but he knew he had nothing of any real monetary value. There was no cash here. No fine jewelry. No credit cards or bank account information. The only possession War truly considered to be his was the white gold 'T' Torrence had given him when she spared him from the violence of her merry men, and he did not ever allow that charm to leave his body.

Of course, he considered as he looked about the mess, that one such as Torrence took only small tokens from her victims, small tokens like a pearl or a very short necklace, though she'd never given him an answer when he asked what that token from War might've been.

Then a thought occurred to him— this terrible pain rushing through his flesh; it sent his human heart into a palpable rush and caused his human chest to tighten. For a moment, he wondered what might happen to this body if became suddenly incapable of breathing.

It was Torrence. His mind always went to her. So very troubling when he'd come here for a mission, and so troubling when he acknowledged how sinful such an obsession was.

He turned to close his door, shut out the daylight, don't look at the sun or parting skies, and he realized the few books he kept on a small

73

table that came with the apartment had also been destroyed.

The spines laid on the floor bent into deep creases and broken. Small pieces of paper, once full pages of poetry and human spirit, littered the ground beneath his feet.

His brows creased tightly. Lips tightened. Chest, still tight. Everything felt wrong, not just physically, but emotionally as well.

And, oh, these dreaded emotions. These indescribable and illogical pieces of humanity and soul that War simply was not meant to have.

He couldn't deny them, though. The words of those books had touched him, and he bent down to retrieve them, to grieve the remnants of the life they once possessed.

Picking up the pages, the pieces of paper ripped and torn into tiny, illegible fragments of words and emotion, War felt like he might cry.

Behind him, a deep voice spoke tenderly. "Hello, Brother."

War turned. He stood quickly. The scraps of paper fell from his loose hands, fluttering through the air around him, and littering the ground at his feet.

"Mecial," War gasped. "Brother, you've manifested."

"Yes," he said, looking down at his hands, at the deep tones of flesh around the tissues and the bones. His brows furrowed. "The skin is the most confounding thing," he said, flexing his fingers. "It's so... so..."

"Confining," War said, and he nodded.

Oh, the flesh. War remembered the first time he'd felt it against his essence, locking the eternal magnitude of his spiritual being inside it.

Manifesting himself, transitioning there, was more painful than vision-adjustment, but once he was attached to the corporeal creation, which resembled his true likeness as close as flesh and bone was able, he found being in a body tantalizing.

Nerve endings, nociceptors, neurotransmitters. Wow. He wanted to touch everything. But he was limited.

Rules. Laws. Orders.

Observe. Silent. Invisible.

Generally speaking, War found the creatures of Earth were peaceful. Four-legged creatures with fur, their souls were so pure. Other creatures had scales and some had feathers. They only did harm from instinct, for survival, for their spirits were not attached to the same type of brain as that of the humans.

Oh, the humans. The creatures taking reign over the world. They were not so unlike other cultures and societies within their world— They were identical in their DNA, their cells, their atoms. All of these tiny, microscopic parts which created their corporeal form as a whole. But they divided themselves. They differed on so much, though really they differed not. Gender wasn't viewed to them as it was to other creatures. Small things like height, a non-issue to those without physical forms, but to these types of cultures, even tiny measurements mattered.

They segregated themselves time and time again, always deciding that someone is better than the others, that those with a certain shade of hair are supreme, that reproductive organs can have a right and wrong size, that brown eyes were honey and superior to blue but that blue eyes were the sky and therefore the most beautiful.

It baffled War and spirits like him. To those in Heaven, all of these physical attributes— the browns, the blues, the greens, the hazels— were beautiful. Works of art that had been divinely created from the invisible ingredients of the universe, and that every single one, for all their similarities, was unique from all others; a marvel. Each living being in this realm, this physical world, a masterpiece of the solar system which housed them and the sacred spirit who'd created them.

There was that darkness still inside these creations, though. War could not get beyond it. Viciously they battled. For each small disagreement— the level of fun had by the golden haired in comparison to the caramel or brown or black haired, the authority of the small statured against the towering, self-proclaimed dominance of the heightened— and then there were larger, deadlier discordances.

These creatures, these humans, they murdered their own kind. The hunted and maimed and tortured the other inhabitants of the planet, spilling their blood, pridefully feasting on dead flesh.

He had hated these facets of them. But in the art, the physical expression and, therefore, the proof of human divinity, oh, what comfort and joy he found in consuming it, even when its house became his downfall.

"Why did you destroy my books?" War asked, looking at the mess at his feet, the mess still in his shaken hands. "What were you seeking?"

"I did not do this," Mecial said, stepping closer. "A human came. A female."

"A female?" War asked. Torrence?

"Yes. One with very fair, curling hair."

Not Torrence.

"I think, my Brother, she was meant to scare you."

"Scare me?" War's brows furrowed. Had he missed a sign from the Lord?

Mecial exhaled. He brought a hand to his chest, still intrigued by the physical reactions that accompanied certain spiritual sensations—spiritual sensations that mimicked human emotions quite closely, but were certainly not such vile traits of lesser beings. "I don't think you're wanted here, Brother. Or maybe the crime's motivation is that you're wanted somewhere else."

War swallowed thickly. Nervousness rushed him in a force of newly-intense emotional pull, and he, like his celestial kin, took note of the physicality of it.

Mecial eyed War in contemplation, but his knowledge of War's whereabouts seemed obvious.

A chill ran down War's spine, sending his muscles into involuntary spasms and causing his skin to prickle.

"Tell me," Mecial spike evenly, "is there somewhere else you'd rather be?"

"No," War said haphazardly. He tried to remain stoic, tried to hide how joyous the idea that Torrence might have wanted him to remain with her made him feel. He tried to hide that was he feeling at all. "I am happy you've made it here," War said more steadily. "But how is it possible?"

"The tear in the sky is growing larger," he said. "It is easier to pass through, which is quite troubling. What other entities may pass into this world from the one beyond it, Brother, and why have you not found the soul to stop it?"

"I tried. I've studied paintings, sculpture, books, music," War said. "Humans... They are unlike my imaginations of them."

"I know."

"No, you don't. They're vicious, Brother. Cruel. Smart enough to inflict cruelty beyond simple violence. It's these physical abilities blended with the intelligence of the soul. Everything must be seen or touched. Proven. They have feelings, gut-feelings they call them, but they do not use them as evidence. Those who follow instinct or feeling or watch for signs are often ridiculed. They do not believe in fate or purpose or in God. Some of them do not even believe in the soul."

"Brother, Brother..." Mecial raised a hand, tenderly slowing War's words. "I am aware of these humans."

"But you have not spent time with them. You have not been their enemy or victim or friend or—"

"Lover?"

War recoiled. "Lover?"

"Do not think that God is unaware of your trespasses, *War.*"

"I simply wanted an identifier."

"An identifier? To whom should you identify yourself?"

"I enjoyed the photography art-form of Andrew Warhola, and I wanted to—"

"To adopt his name? But why, Brother, have an earthly name?"

"In case of interaction. To maintain the image of man, that's all. I did not mean to—"

"To bed the enemy? You did not mean that, Brother, no. Certainly not."

"I have not been bedded by anyone, especially the enemy."

"She is the defiance of Lucifer himself," Mecial said sternly, tone still low for how the words roared inside his human mouth. "She murders, War, and she consumes, and in her consumption she commands the tearing skies."

"Torrence... She can't... She's not—"

"She is, Brother. She is sacrilege; sin and violence and blasphemy. She is the soul you sought out, War. She is the bringer of annihilation, and you have not named her to us."

"The museum..." War whispered, his brows tying together above downcast, distraught eyes. "You sent me to find the soul, and I... I didn't realize... I thought the soul was in the art."

"You misunderstood, Brother." Mecial frowned. "But do not fret. Your job was done just the same. You found one of two necessary souls. I just hope they have not yet found one another. But my presence here, my ability to pass through the tearing sky suggests they have. At least in understanding."

"They..." War's lips parted, his stomach twisted as tightly as it had upon his initial desire for Torrence, for now she had been the key to all of this, to stopping this. "The tape," War said. "Oh, Heavenly Father, Conrad's tape."

"Conrad?" Mecial asked. "The other soul, I assume. What is this tape you speak of?"

"A recording of... of a possession. Subsequent recordings of slayings."

"A possession and slayings, and you did not comprehend what was before you? Brother! I grieve for you, for what this world has done to you, for what she has done to you, and, my dear *War*, I grieve for what God will surely do to you now." Mecial walked by him, looking down on him briefly in despair and disappointment.

Behind him, War heard the sound of the apartment door opening, and he mustered all strength which remained in his fragile form. "Don't..." War whispered, his arms between his buckled knees, shoulders collapsing in on himself. "Don't hurt her..."

"I shall do what I must do to prevent the final sacrifice. For your sake, my darling, naive, little brother, I hope she does not slay the seventh virtue before I find her."

CHAPTER EIGHT
Devotion

"Tor," Wesley said, a smile spreading across his handsome features as he opened the door to her. "Hey."

"Hey," she said gently.

"Is something wrong?"

"No," she said. "I wanted to make sure we were prepared for the next virtue."

"Oh, of course." He smiled, stepping aside so she could enter.

"This is her address." Torrence handed him a slip of paper.

"Okay, great."

"I'll need to see what you're taking," she said, walking by him. "Everything is in the game room still?"

"Yes." Wesley followed her down the hall. "Do we need something more than usual or is this a random check?"

Torrence avoided his question. The answer was simple, tomorrow will bring the death of the seventh virtue so it is of the utmost importance that all is according to plan, but this simple answer was enfolded in the omission of a painful truth.

As she paused at the wall of framed-photos— family portraits, photos of friends and fake-brothers taken in bars and at frat parties, photos of Wesley's life before he met Torrence— she considered all she built with him. She had freed him of the sources of his pain and provided him a fierce and loving loyalty no other person could've given, but if he knew this secret, this lie-by-omission, would he feel the loss of that trust?

79

She did not want to lose her right-hand-man, not when tomorrow was the thirtieth.

Wesley moved into the room while she studied the photos, unlocking gun cabinets full mostly of various knives and machetes, and bringing forth each weapon. As he laid the items out across the tearing felt of an old pool table, he looked to Torrence. He watched her. Studied her face in this moment the way she studied his face in the captured moments of his past.

She stood there in his game room beautifully. Her posture had always been pristine, her hair never lacked sheen despite the conditions of the world now, and her elegant face became more and more attractive with each communion she'd taken. In this physical perfection, she appeared almost angelic, even wrapped in the dirty, torn leather of her black jacket and adorned with the diamonds and pearls of her murder-victims.

How graceful this body truly was, especially considering what it housed, but Wesley acknowledged how purposeful this appeal had been. Just like Conrad's body, Torrence's body was the best disguise for a monster to adopt. How likely would anyone be, including himself, to follow into darkness any demonic mutation that hadn't concealed itself in the trappings of desire?

Though he acknowledged this— the hideousness of Torrence's soul, or lack thereof— Wesley stared at her in utter reverence. Regardless of what anyone said about Conrad, Torrence was Wesley's savior; the destroyer of those who harmed him and the keeper of his Frankenstein heart. She hadn't caused him any pain, and she stitched together the fragmented remains of his soul when she freed him from that pain.

While he may have questioned her actions in the beginning, worried about them, worried for himself in relation to them, Wesley did not have to question Torrence's fidelity. So long as he was loyal to her and to her cause, whatever that might have been before the skies open, then she would remain considerate of and true to him.

It was genuinely all he'd ever wanted from another— this feeling of safety and security. Emotionally, Torrence provided that right away, and after some adjustment-time, he realized her aggression and cruelty provided it physically too.

Her aggression, her cruelty; It provided access to fortune. It was giving even though it was thievery. She robbed people of their wealth, of their expensive possessions, their safes, and of their lives, but she only ever gave to Wesley.

"That one..." Wesley said, his head tilting a bit as he eyed the photoframe Torrence was studying. "Remember the man in the red Corvette?"

"Huh," Torrence mused, letting her hand fall away from the silver. She looked to Wesley. "I can't believe where we were then, and where we are now."

"The skies," Wesley said. "The virtues and the rituals. I wouldn't have thought such things were possible." He extended his hand to her. "I didn't think a lot of things were possible, for me anyway, until you found me."

She took his hand, smiling. Praise shone from her eyes as they consumed every inch of his physical being. So attractive. So loyal. So willing to submit. His reward, a small but comforting lie. "I couldn't have done any of this without you."

As she approached the pool table now, she considered where they were together, and how easily he'd been swayed to join her here.

He'd been a marketing major when she found him, a full-time student working part-time at a music shop, desperate for the love of a woman who simply would not provide it. Now he was the worrisome shadow in a darkened alleyway, the dreadful bump in the night that awoke sleeping couples in their beds.

She thought the same might occur with War, but the virtuous did not carry the same experiences of the jaded, and thusly were not as susceptible to her charms. Perhaps that bit of fear had worked. She was so good, after all, at feigning comfort.

"I took the tape back to Skeet and Jack."

"Took the tape back?"

"They can still use it as a recruitment tool," Torrence said, as she tested the sharpness of the blades in the table. "Even when the Savior is fully risen, he can gain new followers."

"True," Wesley said, watching her examine brass knuckles and clicking locks attached to chains in place. "I remember when we first watched that tape," Wesley said, looking over to Torrence. "I remember the way it crackled and popped. I thought it was going to snap."

"I told you it'd be fine," she said.

"Yeah." He scoffed a laugh. "You're never bothered by anything, are you?"

"What do you have to be so afraid of?" She asked.

He stared at her for a long moment, studying her. Her eyes weren't on his. Her head was lowered. She stared down to the bag on his bed.

"Torrence?"

"Yeah." She grunted more than she spoke.

"Why are you here?"

"Why am I here?" She twisted her lips as if the question disgusted her. "I'm always here."

"You know what I mean. Why are you here now? Before the job? When is it? Tonight?" His eyes flickered from her jerking hand motions to her downcast eyes. "And why haven't you looked at me since we came in here?"

Her chest rose as the audible intake of air passed swiftly through her nostrils. She lifted the gun to inspect it. Holding it in one hand, she opened the chamber with the other. When she saw that the empty slots left by the magnum used at the last sacrifice had been filled again, she closed the cylinder.

Tossing the gun back onto the table, Torrence stood with a hand on her hip and her other rubbing at her forehead.

"Okay, look," she said, dropping the hand from her brow and turning to face Wesley. "This isn't the sixth sacrifice," she said. Her arms crossed in front of her and she finally looked up to him. "After the night in the museum, the mistaken sacrifice, I found another one my way home."

"You... You found another virtue?"

"Yes."

"And you went after him alone?"

"What are you insinuating? I've been at this a lot longer than you have."

"No, you have not," Wesley said. "Petty shit, sure, even murder, way before me, fine. But you never tapped into unknowable, supernatural shit alone. You didn't perform ritualistic killings alone."

She exhaled a sharp laugh. "All killings are ritualistic." She looked up to him, a heat blazing from the usually-blue irises surrounding her pupils, which appeared in this dim light black, crimson red, maroon almost. Swirling as they changed colors, Torrence's eyes pressed against Wesley's flesh a tangible heat. Six victims. Six virtues slain. Six communions taken. He supposed it made sense for such an effect to take hold of her physical being. After all, increased abilities were par for the course of the Awakener and the Savior. "Shall I go through the steps, significance, and spilled-blood of our first night together?"

Wesley's lips opened to reply, but no words came at first. His lower jaw rose and fell, stammering without speaking. Then he closed his lips, swallowed, breathed for a moment. "Tor," he sighed. "I'm serious."

"So am I."

"So you just left the guy's house and found someone else?"

"Yes."

"Found one that easy?"

"I walked all the way home, Wesley. It's not like War's place is next door to mine."

"War?" A lump forming in Wesley's throat caused a slight cough to escape his lips. "I didn't realize you took names."

"I don't, and if I did, it wouldn't be any of your concern."

"But, Torrence, why didn't you call us?"

She shrugged a shoulder, her lips curled with indifferent consideration. "Supposedly I had all of this power after the first communion. I wanted to test it out."

"You want to— And the fact that time slowed down when we performed the ritual didn't prove it?"

"It proved that the ritual worked. Not that it gave me power. I mean, I saw light in places I couldn't have before, and existing light looked different, but that's not really power. That's not strength." She tilted her head a bit as she gazed into his gleaming, honey-toned irises. "What's the point in awakening a demonic savior's powers if we don't get some too?"

"We? Yeah, exactly, I thought it was 'we'. I thought you were sharing this with me. I thought I was something... I don't know... something more to you than just a follower."

"You are."

He scoffed, his hand running over his eye, down his cheek, and around his lips.

"You are." Torrence spoke more sternly now. "I wouldn't share it

83

with you if you weren't. It still affects you. It affects everyone. You don't need to take communion every time to feel the effects."

"What do you mean it affects everyone?"

"Jason and Michael," Torrence said. "Freddy. Anyone caught in that slowed time experiences after shocks. Not as strongly as you do, and you don't experience anything as strongly as I."

"So it would've affected me regardless of you sharing the blood with me or not?"

"Yes. But not to the same extent. The blood comes up from your lungs when we bury the vials, doesn't it? Our brothers don't experience any of that."

"Fine," Wesley said. "So this is the seventh?"

"Seventh and final," she said. "This vial goes—"

"In the center of the six-pointed-star," Wesley said. "I know. I study. I take this seriously, Torrence, because you do."

"I know," she said. "That's why I share it with you the way I do." She smiled.

For the first time this evening, Wesley felt warmth from her. He always took exceptional notice when Torrence felt warm with him, when she was inviting and tender and comforting. It didn't happen much with him, and it happened far less with others, but it was enough to reaffirm her feelings for him, enough to keep him content.

Often he'd consider telling her how wonderful it made him feel to receive such intimacies from her, but the fear of her reaction always prevented him from doing so. The last thing he wanted was to see apathy in her gaze or hear no emotion in her tone when she replied.

He wondered it mattered to her how he felt, what he said, what he had to offer. Perhaps she shared with him because all of this mattered to her. But, then again, maybe it only mattered that he obeyed, that he followed. Maybe this shared communion was a reward for his loyalty and nothing more. He couldn't be certain if he was her right-hand man— a loyal soldier in this great spiritual journey, a great confidante that she could depend on in her pursuit of power— or if he was more than that.

Yes, she was his leader, an entity far greater than any being he'd ever met, but she was also Torrence, beautiful Torrence with raven hair like the waves of a gently rolling ocean at midnight.

Starry were her eyes. Otherworldly blues that were not water nor sky.

Vast galaxies, instead, of black cutting through navy and speckled like flakes of glitter were the golden, silver, and iridescent stars of the great unknown; all lost inside her eyes. These windows to her soul.

Wesley blinked away from her, away from these deifying musings because he could hear very clearly in his mind the words of man as she slashed away at them with a reckless abandon too severe for such an overused term. But fitting it was for she cared not about the consequences of her actions, however potential in that moment they might have been, and she struck with precision when it came to the strength of her attacks, but had no pattern, destination, or goal in mind when she dealt each blow. Just skin. Just flesh. Just bone. Just body part.

"What— what's going on..." Wesley had asked breathily, shocked by the scene set before him as he entered his dorm room that fateful night, over a decade ago now, when he first met Torrence.

"Wesley!" Jessie cried from the floor, a woman standing over her; each of her combat boots on each side of Jessie's ribs.

The woman grabbed at Jessie's ponytail, yanking it, pulling her head backwards toward her own spine and exposing her delicate neck. "Thank you for the proper introduction, Jessie," the woman sneered, bending her knees as she cooed; her voice low and maniacal for how soft it pretended to be. "I'm Torrence," she said to Wesley. "I've been watching you."

"Watching..." He gasped, confused and paralyzed by his over-consideration of the situation in which he'd found himself. Should he lunge for her, for her weapon? Would that only enrage her further? Is she here to hurt, maim, kill, or is she here to rob and burgle but found someone home? No, that couldn't be it for why is Jessie even here? "What is this? Don't—" his voice caught in his throat; words sticking to the air he tried to breathe, but even his lungs felt tight, too compressed to function.

"Don't hurt her?" Torrence grinned, her brows raised above the large strokes of liner which adorned the cat-like lids of glistening blue irises. "Really? Is that what you want to say?"

"I don't..." he swallowed nerves and fear of this new woman down alongside the pain of Jessie.

"I don't think that's what you want to say."

"Wes—" Jessie started, but Torrence cut her off with a thrust of her wrist which resulted in Jessie's forehead smashing into the fake-wood of the dormitory floor.

"Hush down, pet," Torrence said, wrapping Jessie's ponytail into her fist again. "The grown-ups are talking."

"I don't... know what this is..." Wesley stammered over the sound of Jessie groaning and sobbing; heart-wrenching sounds that reminded him almost exactly of her pants and moans the night he found her in bed with his roommate, and tears as tumultuous and violent as the ones he cried for her in the days that followed.

"This is retribution," Torrence said, her brows lifting, shaping her eyes in consideration of him and sympathy for his plight. "Think of me as an Avenging Angel," she said, slipping her free hand and a small object she held in it around Jessie's face. With the object before Jessie's eyes, Torrence pressed a release button, and blade extended swiftly from it, cutting through the air so violently both Jessie and Wesley tensed at the sound.

"An angel wouldn't..."

"Oh, an angel would," she said, pressing the blade softly against Jessie's neck. "The first twelve angels God created were made solely to seek out wrongdoings and requite them."

"Wrongdoings..." Wesley tried to steady himself but his stomach twisted. Rising bile in his throat caused him to gag. He was disoriented, disgusted, and afraid, but an unconscious part of his soul rejoiced at such a perceivable scenario of karma. "Don't," he whispered, pleading but soft. His shoulders loosened and fell, and his knees gave way. Palms on the ground before Jessie, on his knees as if bowing before God, Wesley looked up at Torrence. His eyes glistened with tears. Nose red and starting to run. "Please," he said defeatedly. "Don't."

"Don't?" Torrence's voice, full of pep and high-pitched, slipped easily from her smiling lips, melodic and unshaken. "Fine," she said, pushing Jessie's face more harshly into the ground again.

She rose from her bended-knees, stepped one boot harshly onto Jessie's back and pivoted there. When her back was toward Wesley, she moved away from the sobbing woman on the ground, took her phone from her back pocket, and illuminated the room with its flashlight.

With great effort, Wesley lifted his head. Riddled with sweat and pained, he worried his neck might snap under its weight, but still he looked up. His brows lifted and pulled together. His lips curled. "Dan," he whispered.

"Dan's a little tied up as you can see," Torrence chuckled as she approached him. She'd tied him to a kitchen chair at the wrists and ankles. Tape was slapped across his mouth. He was in only his boxers. "You'll have to pardon his lack of manners right now."

"Dan... I..." Wesley's voice shook now, his head falling, but, God, did it feel good to see the man he trusted, his roommate, his best friend experiencing the hurt and turmoil he'd caused Wesley to feel. The guilt of this caused him to sob.

"Dan!" Torrence screamed and all three in the room with her jumped at the sound. She backhanded him. "Wesley is speaking to you!" She ripped away the tape from his mouth.

Dan groaned, and Wesley remembered how similarly he'd been groaning when Jessie was straddling him right here in this dorm room, right on the couch they shared.

"Fuck you!" Dan screamed.

"No, thank you." Torrence's lips curled in disgust, then she raised her hand, the small the object still open— sharp and glistening— and plunged it down into the flesh between his legs.

Inhuman cries flew from his lips. Guttural sounds of indescribable pain still trying to take the shape of curses.

Jessie screamed. Her shaken hands rose to her ears, and her contorted body curled further in upon itself.

"Don't think you'll be doing much of that with Jessie anymore either," Torrence sneered.

"Fuck!" Dan screamed again. "Fuck you! You crazy bitch! Fuck!"

Torrence backhanded him again. "Watch your language. There are ladies present." Her head tilted, eyes narrowing on him as he sweated and panted and gritted his teeth in agony. "But what am I thinking? Expecting chivalry from you." She scoffed. "I shouldn't expect even the most basic manners much less any sort of respect. You're not the type of man who respects women. You're not the type of man who respects other men. You don't value friendship, or relationships, or boundaries."

Torrence angled her body now so that the bleeding man was at her right, and Wesley, collapsed still on the floor just before the weeping Jessie, was on her left. "Wesley," Torrence said gently. "Tell me, what is the most important human trait?"

Wesley's eyes, puffing and reddening, lifted to meet hers. He tried to form the word "what" but only the first letter was recognizable inside the defeated exhale which left his still-gloriously-pouty lips.

"I'm asking you genuinely," Torrence said, stepping gently across the room towards Wesley, kicking Jessie roughly before she bent down before him. Her hand lifted and he recoiled slowly, unable to muster even the strength it might have taken to instinctively protect himself from pain. "No, no," Torrence cooed, brushing her fingers across a brunette eyebrow, petting the hair there tenderly for a moment then letting her hand flow down the side of his face and brush away a few of his tears. "I'm not here to hurt you. I'm never going to hurt you, and I won't follow that up with the typical promise or swear or assertion that I've never felt this way for anyone before."

Torrence brought her free now to his jaw, the switchblade balanced carefully in her fingers so that its violent edge was a safe distance from Wesley's flesh. "Listen to me, Wesley," she said, raising his fallen head so that he could see her. "You are nothing like these people. You're better than they are. You don't lie and you don't cheat and you don't disrespect your friends or your partners. You are sensitive to the feelings of others. You listen to them when they speak, and you don't just hear the words they use, no, you acknowledge their meanings. You understand them. You understand what they need and what they want, and you give yourself completely to them; committed and dedicated and genuinely appreciative. That's who you are. That's what you do. That's what you offer.

"Someone like this trash behind us, someone like this trash bleeding to death in his own kitchen, well, they cannot see the value in someone like you— the great value in you— because they are so shallow and selfish that can't be bothered with wasting their time on anything but arrogance and egotistical pursuits. They value fast, easy, instant gratification where you value, very naturally and without any attempt or ulterior motive, the development of strong, in-depth, and unbreakable bonds.

"These people," Torrence tsked. "They're barely conscious enough, sentient enough, to be considered human." She gazed deeply into his eyes now; his eyes reflecting her sincerity back to her, an appreciation.

"Thank you," he whispered, tears still falling from his eyes, his guts wrenching still, but he was heard. He was seen. He was understood. He finally felt valued.

"Tell me, darling," Torrence whispered, her delicate voice the only audible sound, even when screams and sobbed filled the air of the small space in which they sat.

To Wesley, it wasn't him and his friend and his lover here with an intruder. To Wesley, it was him, his betrayer, his heartbreaker all at the mercy of a guardian angel. This angel of vengeance. This biblical deity ready to right wrongs just for him; because he was good and because he mattered.

Torrence asked tenderly, "What matters most to you in a friend or a confidante?"

Wesley's brows tightened, pulling together in sorrow and pain, but he choked out one simple word. "Loyalty."

"Loyalty," Torrence repeated as she rose. She kicked at Jessie again, approaching Dan once more, and when she stood before him, she stared into his eyes.

Trembling, drenched in sweat and tears and blood, Dan clenched his jaw. His face turned slightly away from the terrifying figure before him, this figure cloaked in darkness and black clothing, this figure brandishing an illegal weapon still wet with his blood. He stared worriedly at her from the corner of his eye. Doom hung in the air around them. He was about to die, he knew it. Whether she'd let him bleed to death or strike him again, well, that was the fear now. The end of this night was inevitable.

"Would you like to repent?" Torrence asked, lifting the blade and resting its tip against her finger. "Ask forgiveness," she clarified, condescension as clear in her tone as in her eyes.

"Wes," Dan grunted through gritted teeth. "I'm... Sorry..."

"Valiant effort all things considered," Torrence said. "But the question remains..." She turned and looked back to Wesley. "Can he be forgiven?"

Wesley wiped the back of his wrist across his nose.

"Wesley, have you ever forgiven him?"

"I... I just..." The weight of the question hanging heavy on his shoulders, Wesley's head fell forward again, he sobbed. He couldn't lie, but what awaited Dan if he didn't?

Torrence asked more sternly now, "Have you forgiven him?"

Wesley inhaled deeply, the air entering his shaking body in quick pulls of nerves and emotion. Finally, after a long moment, he exhaled an almost-inaudible, "No."

Torrence grinned. A brow arched over one eye. "Very good, Wesley," she cooed. Very good indeed; A kind soul capable of unyielding and unconditional loyalty and love, but still flawed enough a human being to allow Torrence this vengeful cruelty.

She turned back swiftly to Dan, raised the blade and plunged it into him. Once, twice, three times, she'd lost count. He grunted and hollered; Jessie screamed and covered her ears, a sobbing mess on the floor, and Wesley, with his hands knitted behind his neck, whispered, "Oh, God. Oh, Jesus. I'm sorry. God." But he didn't move to stop her. Didn't even consider it.

Torrence moved away from him swiftly. She placed a foot on each of Jessie again, grabbing her hair and resting her head back. "Tell me what to do, Wesley," Torrence commanded as she pressed the blade, still covered in the warm blood of the dying man behind them, to Jessie's throat.

Fear immobilized Jessie. Spit fell from her shaking mouth as she sobbed silently. Her hands gripped at the floor so tightly, her nails split and broke in the pressure of it.

"Do you want to save her, Wesley?" Torrence said lowly. "Do you want to spare her this retribution and go on living in hopeful fear that the next bitch lucky enough to win your love won't fuck your friend behind your back?"

Wesley cried still. He lifted a hand to his eyes and wiped away the blurring liquid. He wanted to see Torrence in this moment. He wanted to see her eyes, her expression. He wanted to watch what she did when she spoke.

She held the blade to Jessie's throat. She wanted to stick it inside the tender flesh of Jessie's neck and drag it through her vocal chords. But she didn't.

"Is that what you want, Wesley?" Torrence asked. "Or do you want to trust me? Trust me with your heart, with your soul. Trust me to keep them safe. Trust me to keep you safe. Trust me to make sure you never hurt again."

Wesley blinked, staring into her eyes still. Before him was a woman who'd betrayed him, and above her was a woman promising to rectify that, promising that it would never happen again. For as unimaginable as its method was, the concept sounded wonderful.

"Trust me," Torrence whispered.

A sob left Wesley's lips in a sharp exhale of surrender. He nodded, and looked away when Torrence slit Jessie's throat.

Wesley watched Torrence with their weapons now. He wondered why she liked that switchblade so much. She insisted on the gun. Insisted Wesley was the one to brandish it. But with its rarity and undeniable advantages, Torrence still kept her blade tucked safely in her boot, and used it to enact almost all of the ritualistic slayings.

He considered that its appeal before the skies opened was found in its legality. Switchblades had been illegal here. Everything Torrence enjoyed was illegal in some way, and it brought him back to that "mistaken" virtue. Wesley hadn't realized she knew his name. He wondered what else about him she knew now.

"Okay," Torrence said, loading items into a duffel bag. "Vials, gun, ammo, chains, locks. I think you're ready." She smiled as she moved toward him. "Of course, I never doubted you," she said, wrapping her arms around him and pulling him against her. "My perfect Wesley. My most devout follower."

"I love you, Tor," he said, accepting her embrace and returning it gently.

"I know," she said, pressing her lips against his neck before she pulled away. "This is it," she said. "Our final night like this."

"What happens after? I mean, not with the whole apocalypse thing. I mean... with us... What happens to us?"

"You're all devout and loyal followers. You'll be rewarded."

"But what about you? You and Conrad, Awakener and Messiah, will become closer than any two souls have ever been. Where does that leave me... With you?"

Torrence smiled, filled by arrogance and love at this concern. "You'll always be with me," she said. "You don't ever have to worry about that."

"I don't want to do this if we can't still be together."

"Nothing is separating us, Wesley, not if we make this wasteland our hellish Eden. Death and destruction stand between us now because the world that exists beneath open skies is not the world we grew up inside. Go get the others. Collect the final virtue. Bring her to the basement. Let us have eternity together here. Help me make this world ours."

Wesley nodded. "I'll get the virtue, Torrence, and I'll bring her to the church for you and Conrad to slay, but know that I don't do it for him or what he promises. I do it for you."

CHAPTER NINE
Collection

Wesley used an old landline phone to call Jason. They were the only two of the merry men who owned such outdated items. Most people had long-since discarded them for smartphones and other such evolutionary inventions, but in these times of unusable cell towers and useless satellites, a rotary phone had once again become a valuable piece of modern technology.

Wesley had always kept an entire room of such antiquities; Modern inventions which could not have been dreamed of fifty years prior but had become outdated in the years between his seventh and tenth birthdays. This was why he had an old, corded phone, and he had been present during a robbery, just after the third— oh, no, he supposed now that it had been the fourth— virtue's sacrificial slaying, during which Jason had become enamored with the old phone that some forty-year-old man tried using to alert the police to their intrusion upon his home.

Police were not as prevalent here in these days as they had been prior to the opening of the sky. Neither were criminals. Grocery store clerks were few and far-between. Gas attendants. Preachers. Artists.

Yes, there were still billions of people on this planet, but perhaps only half as many as there had been previously. Wesley wasn't sure if that had been a product of the chaos which arose when the skies began to part, or if now, with all things considered, he believed in the rapture.

He wondered briefly, as he awaited Jason's answer, if he might have been in heaven now if it weren't for Torrence and her presence in his life, though he had to admit that he made the choice of inaction when she threatened death and evil deed. He supposed he could have stopped her or, at least, he could have attempted to, so perhaps he wasn't that great of a person even before he'd met her. He wasn't sure it mattered, not now that the apocalypse had started and its soon-to-be ruler was wicked. It might have actually been a positive thing for him.

"Yeah?" Jason's voice came crackling through the phone.

"Nineteen-sixty-two Burgess Street," Wesley said. "Three a.m. is the final sacrifice so we'll have to head out sooner than usual."

"Final? Thought this was six."

"Yeah," Wesley said. "So did I."

When Wesley arrived with Michael and Freddy at the modest home, they exited the vehicle in anticipation of their final member. Freddy with his mask on tightly, Michael with his arms wrapped around himself in the frigid air of the night, Wesley with a useless cellphone in his hand merely to check the time; the three men stood in a loose triangle in silence.

A blaring sound came from the street behind them. Closer and closer it roared until its source became visible to them.

"Jason," Wesley gritted, tucking the phone in his back pocket.

The three men watched Jason rush into the driveway on a stolen motorcycle, then dive recklessly off of it, letting it smash into the homeowner's red vehicle. The car's alarm rang out in the night.

"Damn it," Wesley said. "This is the final one, you idiot. If she hears us coming and gets away, Torrence is going to gut us all."

"Don't worry," Jason cooed, patting Wesley's cheek. "Just the three of us." He gestured to Michael and Freddy. "You'll probably just take a good ass-kicking, but she won't kill you, precious one."

"Fuck off," Wesley spat, pushing Jason's hand away roughly.

"I'm playing, man," he shouted over the alarm. "Let's go get this virtue!"

They entered more violently than originally intended, but the noise outside now allowed very little time to creep.

Wesley had wanted to provide a speech to the men before they entered; he needed to explain that this sacrifice would not go as the last five— six— had gone.

This final virtue, its death would incite grander storms, rising ocean levels, tidal waves, hurricanes, tornadoes, hail the size of fists, earthquakes on larger scales; the skies would indeed part fully, as would the earth at their feet, for this virtue wasn't any virtue. This virtue was the seventh of Torrence's ritual and the fourteenth of the ritual shared by her with Conrad. This would take place within the church where Conrad became fully Conrad, where the demon fixed itself to him, and that alone would force the world into systems far deadlier and greater than any apocalyptic encounter anyone had thus far.

Conrad on his seventh audio recording had not licked away the blood of his virtue. He hadn't even recited his incantation as many times. The seventh sacrifice, as completion of a longstanding ritual, took with it all force of the previous six, for their blood still dwelt within the unholy host and called out to it.

The vial, however, was an undeniable piece of this wondrous puzzle, and if Torrence would not be in the position to return it to the earth herself, then someone else would have to.

Wesley wanted to do it; he had done all others— save for one, he acknowledged now— so he knew precisely *how* to do it. There would not be room for error. But he wanted the others aware of its importance, and of Torrence's potentially compromised state, in case he too were compromised or too concerned for Torrence to move.

Ah, well. Something for the car ride perhaps. Not something to worry about now, for this mission was unlike any other. A kidnapping. An uninjured victim. There was much to keep focus on, and the church and its ritual would have to be focused upon later.

When they entered the home, Freddy remained by the door while the others dispersed through its rooms; Michael into the kitchen, Jason the living area, and Wesley up the stairs to where the virtue most likely slumbered.

Tonight there wasn't any unnecessary chaos. No fear tactics. No smashing plates or busting windows. There was no countdown, not tonight. There would be no six minutes of fear before the grand evil herself came into the room.

Tonight was silent and controlled. It required chains and gags and transportation. Tonight their mission was to do as little damage as possible, which was quite uncharted territory for the merry men.

Downstairs, Freddy tried shuffling his feet. He wanted to move into the home as well, wanted to waltz into a sanctuary of safety, see the shock spreading over the virtue's face, and then smirk at her.

He imagined pulling down his mask, allowing the virtue to see his disfigurement, and then snarl something to her about being a monster, a maniac, the bringer of her despair and destruction.

But his confidence had been too shaken by his past. He never moved when the others did. His participation in home destruction was never quite so bold as the others'. They'd grown accustomed to it. They dealt with it. He belonged to Torrence, and because of that fact alone, his position in the band of brothers was never questioned. They found use in him by having him stand guard at the door, and even that sometimes felt useless.

"Fuck!" a voice growled from upstairs, pulling him from his thoughts.

"Don't move!" Wesley's voice commanded.

Freddy peered around the corner of the entryway, watching the wall-mirror's reflection of Michael and Jason. They came from opposite directions but met on the stairs just before the offensive glass.

Freddy didn't mean to look into the mirror. He certainly didn't want to see his face reflected in it. But he saw it, and he could not look away.

Above him, a woman screamed and wailed. A man shouted and sobbed. Freddy heard thudding and yelling, fighting. He heard chains unraveling and a gunshot ringing out.

He wanted to help his brothers, truly he did, but Freddy was frozen, struck by his reflection in the mirror. He hadn't seen his face in years. Hadn't wanted to see it enough to remember what it looked like now.

"Freddy!" Jason roared from above him. "Come on, man! Help out!"

He had to move closer to himself in the glass to get upstairs, and this was troubling. He closed his eyes. Moved swiftly toward the stairs. He turned away from his reflection when he approached it and went to the sound of his brothers' voices. "Okay," he said, a gentle whisper in a sea of chaotic cries.

Freddy never spoke much, but when he did his voice was nearly inaudible. A horrific fire, the result of his own urges for arson, left him terribly scarred, mostly at his neck and lower face.

For quite some time after, he'd stare into the mirror and sob. His reflection, what had always been a source of undeniable arrogance, thereafter served as the driving force of insecurity.

He'd never fostered other abilities in his youth; never tried to find a passion or develop a skill or study a certain topic or discover a talent.

Freddy had been a man of money and of his face, and whenever he acted out in school, the prestige of his mother's name often bailed him out.

As an adult, he could wink his way out of a traffic violation and sweet talk any bystanders of his various "situations" into not reporting him.

All of that ended when he accidentally set himself aflame. He realized all he'd ever valued about himself was fickle and fleeting, but he never supposed how soon it would indeed depart.

Spending years isolating himself away in a large townhouse his parents afforded him, Freddy only emerged to cause the despair he felt and the destruction for which he prayed.

Praying and pleading with some higher power, Freddy begged for release from earthly form for he didn't have the sack to do himself in. He busted storefront windows with the stolen property of his neighbors and he set ablaze anything that would light.

One night, inconsequential for his usual activities, Freddy stood in the blistering cold of a November night, watching his breath become visible in the temperature of the air outside his body; the flaming church a backdrop for the focus of his breathing. He didn't like to see his breath, this visible confirmation that his lungs still operated, for it meant that he was still alive. Above all, Freddy lost any desire to be alive.

Tears streamed down his cheeks as he looked up to the fire, to the chaos he caused, and he asked God why He allowed him to live and to destroy and run amok.

Why, why would God allow such a vial, disgusting, unbelievably shallow person to continue his string of violence? Why wouldn't God strike him down now? Smite him. Here he was, an insignificant man with a ruined body and a sour soul, standing before the house of the Holy Lord God and crying as the flames of hell, by his hand, consumed it.

He collapsed there in the snow. Too weak to even be desperate, too lost to be angry or pitying or sad. "Why, God?" he asked the heavens, his head hanging between his sunken shoulders, his hands between his legs, lazy and loose and turning red where they touched the snow. "Why am I here?" He whispered, his last bit of energy now expelled with the question.

An answer came. Smooth and gentle and understanding. Like the voice of an angel. Was this his salvation?

"No," the woman said, resting her hand on his shoulder. "This is better than salvation."

He looked up to her where she crouched down next to the physical repercussions of his broken spirit. Gleaming blue eyes, dark hair, astonishingly beautiful.

He sniffled. Oh, if this were a year and a half earlier, Freddy would've tried to woo her with every trick in his short-and-shallow-book. Instead, he sniffled and asked her not to look at him.

"No," Torrence said again, and Freddy recoiled from her. "No," she said more sternly, reaching for his cloth-covered chin and jerking his face towards her. "Look at me," she said, "because you're no longer in charge of your life."

"I'm wh—"

"You shut up and you listen," she said, her tone soft but no longer gentle. "You made your own choices for twenty-six years and you fucked up. You fucked up royally. And you didn't even learn from your fuck-up."

His green eyes glistening in the moisture pooling in them, Freddy stared at Torrence in wonderment; who was she, this elegant figure with blue eyes which reflected the flames of the church and appeared as portals between this place and the unholy lake of fire itself, and how did she know what she seemed to know?

"Hiding your face," she said, "is a joke." Her once-violent motions grew softer as she released him from her sturdy grip. "This is not a curse," she said, brushing the back of her knuckles along the cloth he'd wrapped around his mouth and jaw and neck. Slowly she gripped the fabric in two fingers and urged it gently downward.

"No," he started, a shaking hand reaching towards her hand, but he stopped himself. The fear of Torrence somehow stronger than his self-loathing, and wasn't that, the fact that something could outweigh that hatred he had for himself, something miraculous?

"Wonderful," she said, slipping the fabric from his face. She stared for a long moment at the scarring, the damaged tissue, directing all of her focus and attention in very obvious ways to the exact point of Freddy's person that he'd been trying desperately to hide.

"What?" he asked.

"This is a blessing," she said, delicately caressing the twisted flesh. "My God," she exhaled. "You're beautiful."

"I'm... No... I'm not..." He choked, trying to steady himself enough to speak through the tears that still flowed freely.

Torrence's eyes widened and she leaned in closer to him. It felt, to Freddy, as if she couldn't consume his features enough, as if she needed more, as if he weren't hideous and deformed, as if he were as beautiful as she said he was.

"You're the most beautiful man I've ever seen," she said. Finally her eyes left his lower-face and rose to his eyes. "Stop this," she said as she wiped a tear away from him. "And stop this meaningless destruction."

"Are you... You're here to punish me for this? For my crimes?"

"No," she said gently, her lips curling into an inviting and warm semi-smile. "I'm here to save you. Destruction and chaos will continue, yes, but to a great purpose— to a divine purpose."

"Divine like..." He gestured tentatively toward the burning church.

"Absolutely not." She smirked.

"Then... How?"

"I can show you," she said, standing and offering a hand to him.

Standing in this room, this last stop before the final communion, Freddy remembered how pink and crinkled his hand looked when it slipped into the smoothness of Torrence's hand.

He remembered the shame he felt sitting next to her that night in her bedroom, even though she'd been more than welcoming; she'd placed a soft blanket round his shoulders and she'd given him tea and she'd said that there was a special tape she wanted to show him, that this tape would provide meaning to the lifelong impulses toward violence he always had felt.

Freddy remembered that Torrence said he wasn't alone in those impulses, that she'd always felt them too, that her merry band of brothers felt them, and that there was a savior who felt them and who became possessed by a force which explained the importance of these impulses.

Freddy remembered how warm he'd felt there in that room. Even though he was ugly and stupid and shallow; Even though they watched a VHS recording of a young man still in his teens tied back to a chair and handcuffed to it. He was prayed over by a priest and his vitals were often checked by a psychologist, and he spoke in tongues and in Arabic and then French before finding the Latin that remained on his lips throughout the exorcism.

It elated Freddy to see this boy in agony, but it also filled him with jealousy and anger and sympathy. He liked pain, sure, but he didn't like seeing this boy in particular in pain, and he didn't like seeing the boy's handsome face and perfect skin.

A shiver crawled down his spine as he ran up the stairs. An image in his head of Conrad as a grown man, far more handsome than he could've been at seventeen, standing next to Torrence and all of her beauty, and her brothers behind her in their attractive bodies, and how disappointed they all might be to have such a monster as a member of their congregation.

He tried to push it from his mind now. His brothers needed him. Maybe this could be the moment at which he proved himself. He would show them that he could contribute. He wouldn't stand in the corner, sulking. He would not be useless, not on this, the most important night.

Freddy rushed into the bedroom at the end of the hall. He paused briefly, accessing the room. Michael was holding down the virtue as she spit at him and struggled. Jason, wrapped chains around her knees, dodging kicks and flailing limbs.

When his eyes found Wesley wrestling a man for his gun, Freddy lunged toward them, grabbing a clock from the nightstand at their sides and smashing it over the man's head.

It didn't drop the man, but it stunned him long enough for Wesley to regain control of his weapon and use it to murder the man where he stood.

A silence came across the room after the loud gunshot rang out, then the virtue screamed for her companion; devastated and in pain, she was overcome in those few seconds of frozen shock.

Wesley and Freddy aided Jason and Michael. Each man either holding down her trembling limbs or helping to lock them inside chains.

Wesley purposely watched Jason's hands. He did not want to see the woman's face. He certainly did not want to see into her soul through her eyes, find it pure and righteous and utterly beautiful, beautiful in a way not even Torrence with her viciously dark soul attained, and continue to hurt her.

With the virtue's feet bound and locked in chains, Jason took her wrists into his hand and wrapped the rusted metal around them. Michael let go of her body, which was now under the band's control, and plucked the ball-gag from Jason's back pocket. "Here," Michael said to Wesley, handing him the gag.

Staring at the item briefly, Wesley lifted a hand to it. Slowly he took hold of it, wrapping his fingers around it hesitantly.

"What's with you?" Michael asked. "You okay?"

"Yeah," Wesley said lowly, looking down to the shiny auburn hair at his feet. As he took the gag into both hands now, he considered what his brothers might do if he tossed it aside; what they might do if he jerked the chains from Jason's hands and freed the virtue.

"Are you sure?"

Wesley's brows creased. He wanted this because Torrence wanted this. Everything he'd done in the years they'd known each other was because she had wanted it. He liked pleasing her because he liked having her favor, and he wasn't sure how this final communion would alter that favor. Even if she still loved him, how near to one another could they remain?

"Yeah," he said again, more curtly this time. Roughly he slapped the ball against the virtue's tightly-closed mouth, and when she refused to open it, he gripped her cheeks. Forcefully pushing his thumb into one cheek and his middle-finger into the other, Wesley gritted out, "You're dying tonight regardless of what you allow and don't allow, but if I take you into that church screaming, it's going to be worse for you."

Reluctantly, with anger in her tearing eyes, the woman opened her mouth. As Wesley moved the gag back toward her lips, she calmly asked, "Why?"

"Because Torrence isn't going to like it if it looks like we can't handle our business fully." He shoved the gag into her mouth violently. His jaw clenched, then he added, "Especially in front of Conrad."

"I don't think that's the 'why' she was curious about," Michael said. "I think she meant why are we doing this."

"Oh." Wesley looked back down to her. "We're doing this because Torrence wants it."

"Because we wanna run shit when the world ends," Jason added. "Tor does that for us, so we gotta do this for her. You get that, right?"

Wesley stood, rushing his hand over his eye then his mouth. "All right, guys. Let's get her to the car."

CHAPTER TEN
The Awakener and The Savior

The night was calmer than usual. The violet bolts of lightning which typically rained down to earth in violent shocks of broken cosmos were distant now. Hidden behind the clouds, the quiet storm illuminated the parting skies behind the old church with rosy yellows and soft reds. It served no greater purpose than to express itself in these moments of earthly fate; to remind the flock— Savior and Awakener in particular— that energy and power and chaos could be calmed and seemingly controlled.

Conrad stood in the stillness of this night; the last calm moments before his true purpose was revealed to the masses and restored to him.

His hazel eyes gazed stoically at the old church. Run-down now, it appeared so much the same for all its differences — all the differences brought about by him; the veiny cracks sprawling through beautifully stained glass, the two steps leading to its door fallen-in, the broken siding which had been white then but was graying now with age and covered in green, slippery moss.

Regardless of the memories this church conjured within his mind, Conrad felt calm. His spirit was serene inside the olive flesh that cloaked his bones; warm beneath the layers of his black t-shirt, black hoodie, maroon leather jacket. The chilly breeze that pressed against his cheeks and rustled through his dark brown hair was more refreshing than uncomfortable. Soothing like the very hand of fate, it caressed his skin and gentle touches that allowed him a moment of peace. He closed his eyes. Let it wash over him. Let the feeling of a human body truly register to his mind, for after tonight, he would become much more than a person.

Inhaling the dewy breeze deep into his lungs, feeling them expand to capacity, Conrad imagined his body absorbing its essence, taking from it nutrients and life and spirit, and as he released it, he considered the air now filled with the parts of him that were also unseen.

As he opened his eyes, his vision full once more of the church and this new world's hellish, open sky above it, Conrad likened this intake and exhale of air to his intake of the entity all those years ago, but there had never been release from it. No exhale of evil. Only its exacerbation.

Before the entity were thoughts. Only thoughts. There were sensations sprung from ideas, but Conrad hadn't allowed himself even the entertainment of consciously watching the actions play out in a daydream. He often shook his head. Distasteful, these images. He'd known that. He often wondered from where they came.

He was a child when these images started, when they'd flicker inside his mind, but with the brutality of thought came too the talent of the body, so Conrad was able to avoid the drives welling inside of him by exerting them onto page.

First he wrote out short plays, tiny poems. When he was thirteen, influenced by the works of horror masters and coming-of-age tales, Conrad wrote an entire novel based on a young boy who went out into wilderness alone and hunted and pillaged and took what he needed to survive.

It was disturbing, this novel-length ramble of ferocious action and brutal force, and he had never let anyone read it, but he supposed it was better than stealing his father's hunting knife and going into the woods in search of something alive upon which he could use it.

He switched to poetry only after this tale, but even his metaphor and meter, which were perfectly measured and described, discussed ideas that the average fourteen-year-old did not have.

Eventually Conrad's only outlet became music, something that could express his emotions, that could give sound to his desires without voicing them, but he couldn't help his mind from writing lyrical adornments to the melodies.

Those, too, came out violent. Always topics of the repressed and animalistic desires the human psyche typically talked one out of enjoying. It was embarrassing to be so different, so Conrad did not want anyone to know how he was feeling.

The plays put on by his parents' church were safe. School musicals were perfectly fine. He excelled in this creative endeavor as well as he'd excelled in music and poetry and writing, but when he felt akin to an emotion, it was calming; it was something someone else felt, and feeling it with them meant normalcy.

It was fun to play a role, to become a different person, and Conrad's enthusiasm for trading in his own mind for someone else's only intensified his natural talent for acting. Release was there from the emotions which tugged at him, especially when he won roles such as Sweeney Todd, for he could see red blood drip from human flesh and he could laugh maniacally and sing about the enjoyment such sights gave him. But he did not need to feel shame, for the thoughts and the enjoyment were not his own.

One night when he was awake at three a.m., hiding beneath his covers and reading a gruesome tale about a bullied high-school girl who enacted a violent revenge upon her tormentors, an epiphany came.

It wasn't merely Conrad who had these violent impulses; it was innately human. There was violence in the plays, the musicals, the novels. Violence was human, so he explored it more thoroughly.

He wrote poetry and song lyrics. He mastered his guitar with private lessons. He took piano classes, learned the basics of drumming. Voice coaches became as common as school work, and when his voice was as good as anyone on Broadway, he ventured into different singing techniques.

By the time he turned fifteen, Conrad was on stage at school, at church, and at run-down basement-bars. He performed harsh vocals, screaming his violent poetry to nineties' goth kids and drunken bikers.

His acting background and ability to become someone, anyone, no matter how vicious they were, provided an essence to his performances with his band that others simply couldn't achieve.

Conrad, with his angelic voice and handsome face, rolled his eyes back into his head, screamed, growled, and exerted as much energy into the air surrounding his audience as he did into his performance. He was aggressive, but not angry. He was art.

But this was before the entity. This was when those desires were only outlet into his creations. He had hoped the expression and acceptance of them would have released him from the images they so often conjured, but it hadn't.

He still kept to himself outside of the performances, still worked on the set across the stage from the others. He'd watch Dion, who so often played his love-interest in the church plays, and admire her face, her blonde hair, her smile.

Though he wanted to talk more intimately with her, Conrad never allowed himself. He'd attempt to walk over to where she was, always stopping himself before he started, always turning around and working on set or going over his lines alone.

Conrad had always loved her, her delicate features, and her small giggle. He wanted very much to be near to her, to hold her in his arms, to overpower her as she squirmed within them. No. Why must you always go there? he asked himself.

One uneventful day, he was given an answer. Because you want to.

He passed the voice off as simply another thought, but before any entity could enter his body, it would have to speak to him. It did. It whispered to him. It was gentle. It spoke in calming dulcet tones. It told him he was special, that it had nothing to do with his blood or his upbringing, but his soul.

Conrad told no one of this voice which spoke to him. Though he always won the lead spot in his high school's musicals and the local plays held by the community, Conrad was rather shy. An introvert who found an outlet for expression of his soul through artful endeavors and found comfort in groups so long as they were singing in a chorus behind him.

In truth, he excelled at almost everything he did, a feature of special soul the entity told him, and Conrad, who never expressed anything in intimate situations, transcended the expectations of his teachers in public speaking courses. Research and debate intrigued him. He enjoyed persuading people to think his way, and didn't mind the praise from teachers when he never let emotion cloud his logical conclusions.

This wasn't to say he had no emotions or desires for companionship. He simply found it troubling to express anything innately Conrad. He had always wondered if that would change with age, if he hadn't come into himself yet, if he simply had to wait until he had a better understanding of who he was and what he represented.

Encouragement came to him one evening, seemingly from nowhere or from everywhere, from somewhere inexplicable that existed only in a shared imagination of those suffering some spiritual folie à deux, but it was far too audible to be a product of his own mind.

"Speak," it whispered. It spoke. It did not create a thought within his mind.

Conrad's head turned toward the sound, this voice was shallow and soft but unrecognizable.

When nothing further came and no one was visible save for Dion and Corey in the seats below the stage, Conrad shrugged this word off.

He went back to adjusting the paper mache flowers that lined large pieces of plywood, creating the illusion that the players on this stage were not here in this building at this time, but wandering 'round an enchanted forest in the time of the Tudor period.

"Go on," the voice said. "Speak."

Conrad looked about the stage, blinking down to his friends and asking them if they heard it. When they said they didn't, he ignored further inquiries from them, solidifying himself then and there to keep this voice to himself.

For two years, Conrad contained this voice, its secrets. It said it was proud of him for keeping it to himself, that this fact alone proved he was the chosen one, a spirit who would become more than a spirit to both himself and to others.

The voice told him about flocks of people surrounding him, listening to his ministries and converting by sheer belief in him. The voice spoke of another special spirit who Conrad would find eventually and that the two of them together were required for this cause.

The more Conrad trusted this entity, the more he believed what it whispered to him, the longer he kept it to himself, the bolder it became.

Eventually it was more than whispers. It spoke to him clearly. Then it grew to screams and cries, and it began ordering him about when he displeased it.

It did not like it when Conrad was shy around girls he liked. It did not like it when Conrad displayed anything but confidence.

Its chastising wore on Conrad, who felt very confused about when

107

his privacy was important and when it was failure, never understanding the demonic wails of the being when it tried to explain that who he was should be kept secret but that what he wanted should always be expressed— whether desire led him to objects or money or other people.

Wearing on him, the entity seemed to feed off of his suffering now. It was as if any energy spent on it, regardless of its base emotion, empowered it.

When Conrad turned seventeen, it had consumed enough of his vital forces to slip inside his flesh with him.

Once the entity was in his body, Conrad could not keep it a secret. It caused him to do things, to perform acts, that he simply could not stop.

He'd argue with himself in front of people, shouting, "I can't believe you did that! Don't touch her like that!" only to scream back at himself, "I am only acting upon the desires that exist within you!"

And it was true. He didn't want to admit it, but there was no lying to a being that dwelt within his body, his brain.

"I know what's in you, Conrad," the entity whispered inside the skull they shared. "I know what's always been in you. I knew before you were born, before you were even thought of."

"How?"

"I told you. You're a part of something great. Something long-ago prophesied. Something most people of this earth do not believe in. You will show them that the end is closer than they realize."

"The end?"

"Of this world. You are key. Your desires are key. Allow yourself to enjoy them when I enact what you always wished to, then encourage your followers to do the same."

Slowly, Conrad obeyed this entity. When it reached for a desirable woman or set fire to the homes in his cul-de-sac, Conrad trembled. He vibrated in his indecision. Let this happen or fight it.

After so much of this chaos went unpunished, Conrad's worries faded. He did not fight it. He enjoyed it.

Soon, it was Conrad controlling the hands of destruction and despair, and when no legal repercussions followed him, he assumed none ever would.

Spiritual repercussions came, however. When the next play, a church production, held its usual casting event, Conrad felt invincible. He never considered the entity to be a demon, nor did he imagine his new abilities to be unholy.

Conrad's feet shook over the threshold of his church, and when he stood on stage, attempting to read the role of Lysander to Dion's Hermia, his voice shook from his lips in breathless pants. His body jerked when his movements should have been fluid.

The priest of this church was not the only person who noticed these oddities, but he was the only one who knew why they occurred. Quickly he fled the stage area, in search of his Bible, of the rite of exorcism.

When the monologue concluded, so too did Conrad's strength. He fell.

Alone with him now, Dion rushed to his side immediately, wiping the sweat from his forehead with her dress, repeatedly asking, "Are you okay? Conrad? Conrad, what happened? What's wrong?"

The entity had been weakened, affecting his body where it had attached to his muscles and tendons.

His eyes flickered open, fully his for the time in years. He wasn't sure how long he'd have this hold of his own body, though, and in a moment of expression so uncharacteristic for the introverted boy, he whispered gently, "I think… I want to love you…"

A second later, those delicate lips curled around gritting teeth. Conrad pushed Dion away from him, speaking now in the voice of the entity, its essence clinging to his vocal chords. "Get… Out…"

She moved away from him quickly, gripping her neck and chest in a fearful recoil, but Conrad hadn't been speaking to her. He was, again, fighting with himself.

Dion moved closer to him, hesitant but concerned. "Conrad?" She reached a hand to his. "You want to… What did you say?"

Conrad's hands moved away from his head. He lifted his chin. Looked down to her as his head tilted. "I said I want to love you," he said gently, a smile slipping across his bow-shaped lips like a serpent.

"You do?" She smiled at the thought.

"Oh, I do," he said, stepping closer to her.

"And you're okay?"

"Perfectly okay," he said, taking her hands into his. "Perfectly okay with you here, so close to me."

She smiled, rising on her toes to place her lips against his. He allowed the embrace, let his eyes flutter closed as he felt her body nearing his. He wrapped his arms around her waist, delicately urging her nearer still, then he deepened their kiss. His hands moved up her body, passed over her shoulders, took her face in his hands, and as he kissed her, he jerked her head swiftly to one side and cracked her neck.

Stunned briefly by the strength he seemed to suddenly possess, Conrad merely stared down to her lifeless body at his feet. It felt good. The voice rejoiced at this action. Then he walked home calmly, got into his bed, and slept soundly for the last time in a long time.

The entity told him this suffering was necessary, that what happened on stage had to happen, that it set in motion a sequence of events that would lead Conrad to great things. It apologized for what it was about to do to him, but insisted that it would benefit him in the long run.

He laid in bed for days after this, but he never slept; never opened his blinds, never ate. The church had weakened him, his body now almost as equal of the demonic essence as it was his human DNA. The entity immobilized him.

"Conrad," his mother whispered through a crack in the door.

"Go away," he said slowly.

"Honey, you're not yourself—"

"I am more myself than ever I have been."

The door closed gently. Outside it were small voices muttering things akin to, "You see what I mean, don't you?" and "Yes, I saw it at the church."

"My ears are fully mine now, Father," he growled from his bed. Then he chuckled gently, whispering as he laughed, "What can you do to me now?"

Priests came and went. Multiple exorcisms yielded no results. Therapists visited and filled him with drugs but none of them stopped the entity.

Lying in a confused paralysis, Conrad couldn't make sense of this new power or of the power of the entity. It had to be real and separate from him for the drugs did nothing to diminish its presence, and the feeling of the church and the priest's eyes on him was too intense to genuinely bear. But now, as he laid in bed, holy water tossed upon him, prayers sang over him, nothing hurt. Nothing moved him or the entity.

He was locked inside a body that reacted to stimuli or didn't, and there was no way for him to discern what would or wouldn't cause pain or suffering or motion.

As a final resort, the priest asked Conrad's parents to return him to the church, the one place that seemed to have its holy effect on Conrad properly, and when this proposition was posed, the entity, soft and quiet again, whispered a celebratory, "Yes."

"You want in that church again?" Conrad said, his face still buried in his pillow.

"It's where you become you," it said. "Twice."

Conrad walked down the staircase slowly. His hand, elegantly shaped and wrapped in divinely-tanned flesh, reached for the old wooden railing. Hard, cold, splintered in the aftershocks of his exorcism then abandoned, the basement banister had never been replaced. The church had been abandoned after that night, after the prophecy written off by priests as the ramblings of some unholy insect had been sung.

Conrad remembered his limp body as the priest and the psychologist dragged him into the church. They prayed over him. They blessed him with holy water.

The entity bubbled inside him, growling and shaking and vibrating the cells of Conrad's body until it exploded within him a burst of energy.

Conrad's hands moved to his ears, trying to block the sounds of the entity's screams, but the entity was inside his mind with him.

"Stop!" Conrad shouted at the priest, "Stop it! Please!"

His new energy in control now, Conrad fled the priest.

Shocked by his movement, the priest and psychologist stood frozen for a moment before they took off after him.

Conrad went for the exit, but his father was there, holding up his arms and crying, "Please, son, let them do this. It's for your own good."

"It's not!" Conrad screamed, his nails digging into the flesh on his cheek and head as his hands curled around his ears. "This is who I am!"

"It's… who you are…" the entity said weakly.

"No!" Conrad screamed. "Don't leave me! I want destiny!"

"Destiny? Son?" His dad reached for him still, the priest and doctor were closing in on him.

"No!" Conrad shouted, backing away from his father and running down the stairs behind him— his only option for escape.

111

"Where did his strength come from?" The psychologist panted as the three men moved down the stairs.

Conrad ran against the back wall of concrete in the basement. His head pushed into it, hands still digging at his ears, his head, his skull. The entity screamed inside him, and he screamed into the basement.

"Take hold of him!" the priest commanded, holding a crucifix to his forehead as his father and the psychologist took him by the arms.

They tied him to an old chair that remained here from the old Bible Studies days, bounding him at the ankles and the wrists and around his chest.

As they prayed, as the priest performed the exorcism, Conrad felt the entity diminishing, felt it growing smaller and smaller, slinking away, but not back to hell, no, merely deeper inside him.

"I am not a demon..." it screamed as it retreated into his marrow, "I never was a demon…"

Conrad cried out in agony, the essence of this spirit pushing itself inside his muscles, his bones, his cells. His body was not big enough to house them both, and tears fell in streams from his eyes, blood poured from his nose, came up from his guts and pooled at the corners of his mouth.

"Too... much…" He gritted, crying and shaking.

"We are all too much…" it whispered, still seeping into his tissues. "This flesh… cannot house the entirety of our spirits…"

"You're me!" Conrad yelled as the priest prayed. "You were always me!"

"Always…" it said, the last tiny bit of its essence slipping inside Conrad's nerve endings, his brain stem, and becoming one with him. "We are one… We have always been."

Conrad's cries ceased immediately. His head fell forward, blood and tears and sweat dripping from various points on his body and blending together on the concrete floor in an amalgamation of pain.

For weeks after the supposed-expulsion of this spirit from his flesh, his wrists hurt almost as if he weren't permanently bound to the rickety old chair in the church's basement. He could smell the mold, hear the dripping of a leak in the room's far left corner; His mouth forever held the iron taste of his own blood.

Supposedly he had been freed of the separate entity inside him, but he knew better. He knew the entity wasn't present, not as the entity, but in the ritual in the basement of church, something had happened to it, happened to him, to them together.

They thought the demon had fled, but Conrad was the demon, and he was whole once more.

Here in the basement now, Conrad stood where the rickety chair had been. Long-since decayed, only soft hunks of wood remained of the old piece of furniture. He looked at the wall, saw the blood where he had run into its concrete. His head tilted slightly.

"Conrad," Skeet said.

"They are here," Conrad finished for him. "I know. I can see the virtue."

Wesley came down the staircase first. Alone. He paused on the final step, eyeing Skeet then Jack then the figure in the middle of the room.

"We have the virtue," Wesley said.

"Fantastic," Conrad answered.

Wesley stared at him for a moment, this figure of unholy perfection who would take his leader away from him. "You want her down here, huh?" he asked, refusing to hide any aggression that dripped from his lips along with his words.

"Torrence wants her down here," Conrad answered gently, never moving.

"Yeah." Wesley scoffed, turning to go back up the stairs. He yelled for his brothers as he started up, the he paused. Turned. "Conrad?" Wesley's eyes narrowed.

"Yes?" He replied smoothly, elegantly.

"This entity… It was never separate from you. That's what you meant on the tape, isn't it, when you said, 'you were always me.'?"

Conrad looked over his shoulder to Wesley, and nodded.

"How did it— You— How did you find yourself? I mean, if we are all great spirits who can't fit entirely inside our bodies, how do we find the rest of us?"

"Your thoughts," Conrad said, "are the clearest communication you have with your soul. Speak to yourself without attempting to answer consciously, and you'll hear your higher self."

"So, the voice you heard, it was your mind? It was auditory hallucinations? The medicine didn't work on you."

"The medicine didn't work because it was not a hallucination. It was me. I was allowing my thoughts for the first time. I wasn't trying to control what I thought. I let my desires come through, and I heard my true self within them."

"But how did it start? Where did it come from?"

Conrad turned now. "You don't trust me? You don't trust that Torrence trusts me?"

"You don't know Torrence."

"Not the way you do, and you'll never know her the way I do," Conrad said. "We are not competitors. None of us in this room are in some way compared to any other. You love Torrence. You love her in a way the others can't. You fear losing her. You won't." A gentle smile spread across his plump lips, perfectly shaped, rising naturally upward at their corners and bow-like. "Where is Torrence?"

"She never comes early," Michael said from behind Wesley, eyeing this divine-like creature before him, wondering if the devil swung both ways, and what he might have to do to win such favor with him.

"Oh, she doesn't?" Conrad asked, the gentle smile still present on his bow-shaped lips. Eyebrows the color of caramel raised over eyes of burnt umber. "Why is that?"

"Who are you to question Torrence?" Wesley's teeth ground inside his curling lips. "Wouldn't you be up shit-creek without her?"

"You mistake my curiosity for judgment," Conrad said sweetly, delicately; his voice as calm and smooth as his demeanor. How odd to remember the animalistic growls on the audio recordings and assign them to this figure. "I merely want to know her," he added, "in every way."

"She thinks it's scarier," Freddy said meekly from the stairs, his eyes only looking up as far as Conrad's abdomen, at his folded hands there.

"Scarier?" His head tilted.

"She likes the idea that we wreck the place," Jason said. "Throw people around, show 'em our knives and gun and shit. They get real scared, man. Terrified. They shake and squirm. One guy pissed his pants." Jason snorted. "But then when they realize that it ain't just us, that we ain't the big show, that something even worse is coming, well, Torrence likes that. And she likes being the something worse too, you know?"

"The something worse," Conrad said. "Fascinating."

"She is," Wesley said, his shoulders still squared. "And we don't need you to verify it."

"This hostility toward me is very admirable. It represents your fierce loyalty to your leader. That loyalty to her, *precious one*, shall be rewarded in ways you couldn't even imagine."

"Yeah." Wesley's jaw clenched around his curt words. "Thanks."

"Come now," Conrad said, "we're all here to serve the same great purpose." His eyes flickering to each of Torrence's brothers before lighting on Wesley again and staying there. "This is the intended sacrifice, is it not?" He nodded to the covered body held between Jason and Michael.

"Yeah," Wesley said, walking down the stairs. The others followed.

Conrad stepped aside, extending his arm to the center of the room.

"There," Conrad gestured toward the large indentation in the center of the concrete floor.

Looking to his brothers, Wesley nodded toward the same, granting them permission to follow Conrad's lead now.

The men near the destination with the virtue between them, her chained feet shuffling in tiny motions.

Michael let go of her arm, lifted her legs at the ankle, and he and Jason laid her down on the indicated spot.

Wesley moved to her now, walking by Conrad, his eyes never blinking, his body square and assertive. Lowering his hand to the gun in his jeans and gripping it, Wesley wrapped a fistful of the cloth into his palm and pulled it away.

A woman's muffled scream pushed through her lips, sliced in half by the ball gag shoved in her mouth and locked head. She sobbed. Weak and fearful, her body had collapsed into itself the broken-concrete and dirt floors of the church basement. Short, curling tendrils of sweat-soaked hair fell over her eyebrows. Her knees were buckled, tucked behind her, beneath her. "Oh, God," she whined against the gag. "God,

115

why?"

Conrad stepped slowly toward her. Bending down, he petted her head. Wrapped one of her curls delicately about his forefinger and marveled for a moment over the streaks of blonde inside otherwise brunette hair. "'Why', my darling, is quite an easy question to answer. You see, you represent goodness, divinity; virtue really, a specific one. Your death shall be the sacrificial cure to charity, and charity, my dear, is the seventh virtue we shall slay. Well, the seventh virtue slain in this, the second and final ritual."

"Second?" Jason, who never retained more information than his specific order at any given time, asked.

"Oh, yes," Conrad answered, still looking at the sobbing woman. "The Awakener must commit seven slayings and so must the Savior."

"You've done yours already, huh?"

"Indeed. And now we await your master to complete our shared ritual in the completion of her own. The sky shall open broader, each side a separate entity from the other, and heaven shall be visible to those still alive upon earth, but so too shall hell be visible at their feet, for the world shall split in two and those burning within the fires of hell shall bear witness to those in the ecstasy of heaven."

"What—" The woman gasped. "Heaven... Hell..."

"You, my darling, will be the one who sets them free."

Above them, floorboards creaked; a slow-paced click, click, clicking in time with the whining wood.

"It's time," Michael said.

A large smile formed on Skeet's lips. "She's coming."

As she stepped onto the broken concrete of the basement, Torrence rounded the staircase to enter the room. There she stood for a long moment; blue eyes glowing in the dimly lit room, black hair blending into the surrounding darkness rendering her visage an overwhelming entity encompassing the entire space around her. She was beautiful, bright. Her stance was defiant and dominant.

"Torrence," Wesley whispered.

"Torrence," Conrad said as he rose. He moved cautiously toward her, eyes locked on hers. "My name is Conrad Stewart."

"I know who you are," she said. "I can't thank you enough for what you've given me."

"Oh, no, it is I who should be thanking you."

She stared into his eyes, smirking. She knew it to be true. A savior needed an awakener.

He nodded, turning his body and extending his arm into the room invitingly. "I haven't touched her. No one has. She is entirely yours. As ritual dictates."

Approaching the woman, Torrence lifted her chin, creating an even higher vantage point over the virtue.

"Hello," she said as she bent down. Her legs parted, taking up as much space as their length allowed, and she rested her forearm on one knee. Something held in that hand where it dangled nonchalantly. She sat her chin in the other hand, her elbow on her knee. She smiled. "I'm Torrence."

The woman sobbed, eyeing Torrence, nodding, shaking.

"Have you heard of me?"

The woman nodded, still crying.

"Good, then that should save us a lot of the whys." She moved her face away from her hand, lifting the dangling one upward and staring at the item within. She pressed a button. Released something from it. A blurring rush of silver sliced through the air. Shivered ran down the spines of her compatriots.

Torrence moved the knife slowly toward the virtue's face, grinning as she watched it recoil. "Now, now," Torrence cautioned. "Don't move," she said, pressing the knife against the virtue's cheek then slipping it under the leather belt of the ball gag. "This is very sharp."

With a great upward thrust, Torrence successfully cut the leather, though she brought with her forceful yank the woman's head. It fell back against the conference roughly, and Torrence tsked. "Now that was painful for no reason. You'll want to watch that this night. We can't risk you dying of a swollen brain." Torrence patted the woman's cheek. "What's your name, Miss?"

"L-Lisa."

"Well, Lisa, I must thank you for how you've lived your life. I never thought I'd appreciate do-gooders, but without you none of this could be possible."

"This?" She stammered.

"We're going to bring hell to the earth," Torrence said. She grinned.

Removing a vial from her boot, Torrence said the evening's incantation.

"Wrath cures charity." She raised the vial to the flickering light in the room.

The six men— Wesley, Jason, Michael, Freddy, Skeet, and Jack— moved into their assigned positions, each a respective tip of a six-pointed star.

The virtue at their center, the Savior there with the Awakener, the vial; on its surface was the dreaded horned serpent, three triangular points spreading from each side of its curling body, and now, on this vial for this virtue, was the triangle atop it.

The flickering light cast the demonic figure onto Torrence's forehead as she closed her eyes, repeating, "wrath cures charity. Wrath cures charity."

The church around them shook, signaling to Torrence that the violet lightning spread across the open sky as it swirled around the church in deadly hues of the flaming fires of hell. She could feel the heat of it, the yellows and reds and burnt oranges, and when her body began vibrating, falling out to the virtuous blood before her, she whispered, "with this offering of virtuous blood—" a large crack hit the church, knocking out the power. "I invoke the violet!" Torrence screamed, stabbing the woman, her demonic vision unobstructed by the loss of light, for the virtue glowed brightly still within the body.

Torrence tossed her switchblade aside, reaching her hands into the torn flesh of the virtue and throwing it into the air.

She rose quickly, recreating that sacred figure from the vial with the blood.

Twisting and swirling in the air, the blood moved in-time with Torrence, no longer slowed by the initial sacrifice of virtue. After the shape of the seven points took form, bursting from all sides of the Savior's Serpent of blood, the liquid, in midair still, collapsed in on itself.

In anticipation, Torrence's eyes stared on the blank point in the air. Her lips parted and a small, sharp breath escaped them. Taking a step closer, she reached a blood-soaked hand towards the point. When it connected to the correct spot in space, Torrence felt it. A bolt of electricity surged through her finger, down her arm, and into her body.

It tingled, itched. Vibrating as it entered her, it pulsated strange sensations out into her limbs, her flesh, the pores of her face, and the delicate wrinkles around her eyes, though these tickling energies of correction were not the goal of this light.

In search of something, it seemed, traveling through her physicality as if on a mission, but where its destination was, Torrence wasn't sure.

She looked down at herself, almost expecting to see this tangible force as it flowed through her being.

Instead, a burst of light illuminated the space. It sprang forth from her, from the center point of the blood-symbol in the air, from the virtue itself, enveloping the air, the room, and its habitants in blinding white pulses of energy.

Wesley couldn't see anything; when he tried to open his eyes, the light forced them shut again. Too painful to observe. But he could hear, and over the high-pitched whistle of the white light, Torrence screamed.

Painful, almost. Bloodcurdling for certain. Loud and echoing and absorbing into the space of the room just as the light was; touching everything, caressing her brethren.

Visual and audible became physically felt, as if the spirit of the universe broke through the channels that separate parallel realities and exerted all of its power into simply making itself known.

As quickly as it'd come, the light vanished. Flowing from the center point where the blood had been, it bolted into Torrence's chest like a bullet from Wesley's gun. It hit Conrad in the same manner. It focused on the two of them where they stood above the bleeding woman, fleeing the corners of the room as if their bodies were absorbing it all, filling only the space they shared now, but still dripping tangibly over the bodies of the other men inside the room.

Wesley felt the flesh of his body shifting into a new, perfected state. Old injuries that never fully healed and still sometimes plagued him tingled within his bones and then were no more.

119

He took no time to truly experience these things for he was far more concerned with Torrence and whatever the blood had done to her. He wanted to reach for her, to take hold of her, aid her, comfort her, but the energy field surrounding her would not allow him near enough to do so.

Still, he felt a oneness within his body, a blending of the mind and the body so that the two were no longer separate entities which could communicate, but became one and the same being.

It was as if his mind no longer needed to communicate to his body. Neurological signals seemed slow to him now. Everything existed within his cells impeccably, synchronized and smooth.

"Tor?" He gasped as he tried to take hold of her, barely noticing registering the painful shocks of the forcefield of light as it pushed his hand away from the three figures in the center of the star. "Torrence?"

"Whoa," Jason said from behind him, noticing how alluring Wesley's voice was, how illuminated his skin had become, how thick and soft his hair suddenly seemed. Then he looked down and noticed that his hands were shapely and soft.

"What the fuck?" Michael gasped, meeting Jason's eyes. "Dude, your eyes are—"

"Holy hell," Jason said. "Yours, too."

They turned to Freddy whose eyes stared at Torrence's body surrounded in the bright, virtuous. He hadn't noticed any of these changes, these improvements to their bodies, but he felt the pressure of eyes upon him and glanced over to his brethren. "What?" he whispered, then he reached for his throat, his lips.

Freddy remembered the image of himself he'd compared to the boy within his mind that night, and he remembered the scars on his hands which had been wrapped around a Santa Claus shaped mug, and here in this room after the great white light, he quickly brought his hands before his face. He nearly fainted in the discovery that now their backs had been healed and smoothed, and when he flipped them to see his palms, his fingerprints were returned.

They began to acknowledge, one-by-one, that this strange light encompassing Savior and Awakener, affected everyone else in the room as well. Blemishes vanished. Scars healed. Minor cosmetic differences formed; the tightening of slightly sagging jowls, cheekbones lifted, jawlines became sharper, the bumps of broken noses and the puffiness of eyes all leveled and straightened and blended beautifully into the skin of the faces.

"The vial," Skeet yelled. "Someone insert it into the Star!"

Michael and Jason both lunged toward the center-point of the room, but the force of the light was too powerful, even with their increased strength.

"Shit," Michael cried, his face turning away from the light. "Fuck, it burns!"

"Just get it!" Skeet yelled, trying himself to reach for the vial at the Savior's feet.

"I'm tryin'," yelled Jason, the skin of his cheeks rippling in the force of the winding wind-force swirling around the two figures in a controlled chaos of a great thunderstorm trapped inside the church. "Damn it!"

Jack remained on the ground and crawled backward toward the storm of energy. Using his foot to kick into the light, he struck the vial on his fourth attempt.

The vial rolled closer to Skeet and Michael. Both men reached with their smooth hands, their palms free now of calluses and cuts, slapping against the cracking ground and shaking dirt of the floor in a blinded effort to find the vial.

"Yes!" Skeet yelled when he took hold of it, even his cries under the influence of the rewarding energy sounded as a great melody within it. "Help me!" he wailed, trying to stand. "The Star!"

Michael gripped Skeet's shirt with his great hands, tugging him, jerking him away from the energy field which threatened to swallow the entire church and its contents into the swirling vortex of its existence. "Fuck!" Michael yelled. "Shit!" He gritted his teeth, planting his boots into a cracked hunk of concrete and using it as a counterweight.

Skeet was tossed across the room by the impressive force of

Michael's throw. "Fuck." He panted when his face smacked off of the ground, but he scrambled up, stumbling and staggering toward the stairs. "Help, help!" he cried. "If I can't make it—"

"Here," Freddy said from the safety of his hiding spot in the corner. He wrapped an arm, now healed of any pain or wound or scar, around Skeet's back, and tightened his other hand around Skeet's clenched fist, securing the vial inside in.

"Go!" Michael and Jack were both crying, trying to block the blinding light from their eyes.

"Run, dude!" Jason screamed, lifting his hands to his ears. "Fuck, this wind! Fuck! Get the Savior his power! Go!"

All men, beautiful and perfect and seductively appealing, now cowered, even in their divine-strength, in awe of the power that had been passed to them— rewards for their devotion, tools to be used in further recruiting, in corrupting, in bringing to this hellish brood the souls of those who remained saved by God's grace. Oh, yes, with these features, the men could draw hundreds of thousands of the earth-bound to Torrence, to Conrad, to the anti-angels and the end.

"Tor," Wesley breathed, raising his arm over his eyes to shield himself from the blinding virtuous light.

It had been slain. It twisted through the air. Its once pale hues of pinks and blues twisted and glistened and seemed to shift from specks of star-like glitter to the sparks and flickers of hell fire.

Deeply red, burnt orange and yellow, the virtuous light now corrupted by the sin for which it had been sacrificed, filled only the space surrounding Torrence and Conrad and the fallen woman.

From where she remained bleeding on the floor came upward pulls of blood and tissue; fragments of broken bone and torn flesh all ripped away in the force of flowing energy.

Above ground, Freddy and Skeet rushed toward the sacrificial burials. The vial in their held-hands shook and vibrated, calling out to the blood in the dirt.

The buried vials reacted the same, shaking and rising and attempting to reach the seventh piece of its sacrificial Star.

Torrence's head was thrown backward, as was Conrad's. The two figures— The Awakener and The Savior— bound together by the flowing light which fled the dying virtue, were held up only by the pull of this spiritual power. It wrapped around their arching backs, slipped inside their lips, their noses, their ears and eyes; it connected them at the waist, following into their rib cages and tugging at each of their bodies, keeping them upright in a force of energy that would've otherwise collapsed them.

"Tor!" Wesley cried, still trying to crawl towards her. "Oh, Tor! Tor! God!"

"Wes!" Jason yelled. "Don't touch her! Don't touch that light!"

"It hurts!" Jack said. "Even with this new strength!"

Wesley didn't care. He reached for her again. Tried to see her clearly. He felt his power rushing through his being, felt it tingling his flesh and pumping in his veins. "Tor!"

"Holy shit!" Freddy gasped when they approved the gravesite.

"The vials!" Skeet yelled. "Oh, The Savior calls to them! They feel the Savior's power!" His knee gave out. Freddy tried holding him up, but he pushed the vial into Freddy's hand. "Just get it in the center," Skeet panted. "Shove it into the dirt!"

Freddy nodded, rushing over the raising vials. They shook more intensely as he drew near, and when he fell onto his knees in a quick rush of action, they began to glow.

"Wait!" a voice cried from him.

"Who the fuck are you?" Skeet shouted from Freddy's other side. "No!" he screamed. "No, no! Fuck you! Fuck you! You're too late! Do it, Fred! Do it! Complete the Star!"

"My child!" the other voice wailed. "I am the angel, Mecial. This is my Brother, an angel known to humankind as War. We are here to assist you, and all of the world! Trust us. Do not do this! Do not! God will reward you if you follow us! Please. Move for God in Heaven!"

"Sorry." Freddy smirked, turning back to the shaking vials, an image of Torrence filling the blackness of his mind. "I already have a God." He shoved the final vial into the center of the six-pointed Star.

"Yes!" Skeet screamed. He laughed over the cries of the angels. "The Savior is risen!"

At the exact moment of the completed Star, the virtuous light,

123

now entirely fire and flame, released its grip on Torrence and Conrad. Their feet came back to the ground; their shoes pressing down into the sacrificial blood of the seventh dead virtue.

The light flowed around their bodies in search of their mouths and eyes and noses. It absorbed completely into their beings. They tasted it, iron and white-hot, and breathed it in like the smoke of fiery brimstone.

Wesley stood. He saw bouts of Jason and Michael and Jack rising on the other side of The Savior and The Awakener.

Torrence's head, which had still been thrown back, was released finally from the grip of the ritual. She lowered it slowly, gently. She blinked, adjusting to her new sight, and breathed in the scent of death and destruction and thunder and the lightning.

The skies were opening all across the globe now. Violet bolts of lightning illuminated the darkness of the night. It was the end of days.

As her head leveled, so, too, did Conrad's head level. They stared at each other for a long moment, their eyes blinking lazily, lovingly, and their chins tilting in the beauty of their sights; Awakened finally and becoming conscious again.

Down the steps came Freddy then Skeet, still alive in their newly absorbed power, but broken from the fall.

"Fuck you." Skeet laughed behind Torrence. "The Awakener is here. The Savior is risen."

"Torrence," a weakened gasp came from the same place as Skeet's maniac laughter behind her.

She turned her head slowly, looking over her shoulder in the recognition of this voice. Her irises like raging fires inside the midnight black of her sclera.

"The virtue," Mecial whispered, looking sympathetically at the blood-drained woman at Torrence's feet.

"Oh, God," War exhaled, falling to his knees. "Oh, God. I'm sorry. I'm so sorry." Weeping, his hands fell to the concrete. His sobs were accompanied by the villainous laughter of Skeet, of Freddy joining him now, of Jason and Jack and Michael.

"The mistaken virtue," Wesley said, drawing his lip into his teeth. His eyes teared when he looked back at Torrence.

She stared at the angels— one standing stern but powerless in this moment now— the other, her tender companion, her War, who continued to cry, "I didn't know. Oh, God. I'm sorry. Torrence. I didn't— I didn't know. I'm sorry. God, forgive me. I'm sorry."

After a moment, Torrence turned back toward the final sacrifice, toward Conrad, but he no longer stood across from her.

Staring at her, awe-stricken and lovingly devoted, Conrad lowered himself to his knees. "My Savior," he whispered in admiration and astonishment. "I am your Awakener, your humble servant."

Torrence smiled gently, placing a hand on his cheek and petting him.

"Oh," Conrad breathed, closing his eyes in appreciation of this demonic approval. "Oh, my Savior." He looked up to Torrence. Her raven hair flowed around her glowing face, her eyes of fire illuminating all that bore witness to her returned-power. She was divine, and she was beautiful; she was perfectly possessed by her own restored evil. "Torrence," Conrad whispered, "My God."